Destrawn has been second of the Aerasceatle clutch for a little over a year. Under Chieftain Kinsey's rule, Fate has begun smiling on them, and some of their people have found their mates. While Destrawn is happy for them, he doesn't think Fate will bring him his own any time soon. He doesn't consider himself good mate material. He's too dominant, controlling, and some would even say overbearing.

When Destrawn heads to the nearby Maven vampire coven to hear news that could be too dangerous if voiced over the phone, he discovers he's wrong. The vampire giving the report regarding the paranormal hunters descending on their area—a seasoned and savvy tracker named Sorbin—is his mate. Ready or not, Destrawn knows he has to accept him. After all, he only gets one, and if he doesn't accept Sorbin, the vampire's ability to feed will be compromised, which would lead to his death.

Can Destrawn learn to surrender to his mate's needs while remaining strong enough to keep everyone safe?

Surrender to the Vampire
Copyright © 2021 Charlie Richards
ISBN: 978-1-4874-3185-3
Cover art by Angela Waters

Published by eXtasy Books Inc or
Devine Destinies, an imprint of eXtasy Books Inc

Look for us online at:
www.eXtasybooks.com or www.devinedestinies.com

Surrender to the Vampire
A Paranormal's Love Book Thirty-Two

By

Charlie Richards

DEDICATION

Surrender to what is. Let go of what was. Have faith in what will be.
~Sonia Ricotti

CHAPTER ONE

Waking from roost, Destrawn rose to his feet. He stretched his arms over his head and arched his back. Spreading his wings, he groaned as he twisted and turned, working out the kinks from his sleep.

Destrawn didn't know how it happened, seeing as he was a stone statue during the day, but he always woke up stiff.

After cracking his back, pulling a deep sigh from him, Destrawn lowered his arms and rested his hands on his hips. He peered down from the roof at the activity on the large patio below. A number of human and shifter mates, as well as a bonded gargoyle or two, bustled around the space.

Cocking his head, Destrawn tried to remember what they were prepping for.

"Wow, they've gotten a lot done for the New Year's party."

Upon hearing Head Enforcer Sethnos's Spanish-accented voice, Destrawn turned and stared at the giant, powder-gray gargoyle. He had joined the clutch at the same time as the other male. Destrawn was slowly coming to know his new clutch-mates.

When a big shift of power had taken place in the clutch, the gargoyle elders had sent missives to other clutches to see if there were any acceptable gargoyles interested in taking a leadership role. Destrawn had applied for the position, and after a number of interviews with not only Elder Vermidian but newly appointed Chieftain Kinsey, he'd moved from a clutch in upstate New York. Sethnos had joined them from a secluded clutch in the mountains near Mexico City.

Good thing, as a paranormal, they didn't have to worry about securing passports or green cards.

Destrawn figured Sethnos had to still be dealing with a bit of culture shock.

Pulling his attention to what the other gargoyle had said, Destrawn nodded. "Right. A party on New Year's Eve."

As a creature who lived anywhere up to two millennia, Destrawn didn't understand the desire to celebrate when one year ended and another started. Coming up on his sixth-century mark, he found that the years had begun to run together. The only thing that truly changed was human technology, which made it either easier or harder for paranormals to hide in plain sight.

From what Destrawn had gathered from the excitement in others' voices when they spoke of the celebration, it was a new thing to the clutch. After hearing some of the horror stories of what the remaining members had been dealing with under their old chieftain, Destrawn understood why the healing members would need things such as this to cheer them. For the smaller, weaker gargoyles, their lives had been hell under ex-Chieftain Grecian. They'd been little more than slaves.

Over a year before, Chieftain Kinsey had only been an enforcer. Due to the prior chieftain's skewed views on fated mates, the clutch's second—who happened to be Kinsey's sire—had damaged his bond with his fated mate—Wendy. That had weakened the second, allowing Kinsey to easily best him and making it possible for Kinsey to challenge the chieftain. In the presence of a gargoyle elder, Vermidian, Kinsey had won, taking over the clutch without bloodshed.

After hearing how Grecian had treated the clutch's smaller gargoyles, Destrawn had wished he could have inflicted a little bloodshed on the man.

Destrawn's stomach rumbled, pulling him out of his

thoughts. A glance around told him that Sethnos was already winging his way off the roof, heading in the direction of his suite. While stretching his arms over his head, Destrawn started to do the same.

Spotting Rundin carrying a box across the patio, Destrawn hummed and rubbed his neck. The small tan gargoyle gave a damn good neck massage. Destrawn had utilized his services more than a few times.

As Destrawn turned away from the sight and jumped into the air, catching an air current with his wide black wings, he thought about interrupting Rundin for fifteen minutes. He knew the little gargoyle wouldn't mind working on his neck a bit. Except, while landing on his third-story balcony, Destrawn thought about his last interaction with Rundin two days before.

Rundin had looked at him with hero-worship in his eyes. His hands had lingered just a little too long on his neck ridges. He'd even appeared to be blushing, which was tough due to a gargoyle's thick hide-like skin.

Destrawn figured it had something — or everything — to do with the light scent of Rundin's arousal filling the air.

He's getting a little too attached to me.

While Destrawn didn't mind being friends, and even friends-with-benefits, with a clutch-member or two, a sixth sense he always listened to told him that Rundin wouldn't be able to handle a relationship like that. The look in his eyes and the blushes told Destrawn the truth. The smaller gargoyle would end up looking for commitment.

Having no intention of leading anyone on, Destrawn silently vowed to stay away from the other male. He would have to turn down future massage offers. His pulsating shower heads would have to do.

With that thought in mind, Destrawn headed into his suite and did just that.

Destrawn strode from his suite a half an hour later. Moving swiftly, he carried a huge mug of coffee, compliments of the machine he'd set up in his room. It had been a going-away present from a few friends in his old clutch.

They'd known how much Destrawn loved the high-end coffee his last clutch's kitchens offered, so they'd set him up right.

Taking a sip of the steaming brew, Destrawn enjoyed the strong roast flavor with a dash of peppermint creamer. He licked his lips and smiled. Then he took a larger swallow.

Yeah, that's about right. Maybe there is a reason for the holiday season after all. Creamer that tastes like candy canes. Yum.

Destrawn made his way to the dining hall, nodding in greeting to those he passed. The Aerasceatle clutch wasn't large, by any means. It only contained twenty-seven members, and that included mates as well as the gargoyles and their vampire mates who currently resided at the coven.

"Second Destrawn."

Hearing his name, Destrawn paused just inside the dining hall doors and peered around. He spotted Tracker Lionad hurrying toward him. Waiting, Destrawn wondered what the mated gargoyle needed first thing in the evening.

"Sorry to disturb you before breakfast, Second Destrawn," Lionad stated, dipping his head in deference and not looking him in the eye. "But Chieftain Kinsey asked me to find you as soon as you appeared from roost."

Destrawn knew that Lionad's subservient actions was a remnant of the way underlings had to address the inner circle under Grecian's leadership. While Destrawn knew he was a dominant son-of-a-bitch, that attitude was not needed there any longer. He recalled how Chieftain Kinsey had encouraged them all to remind their people of that fact at every opportunity.

Lifting his hand, Destrawn crooked his forefingers. "Tracker Lionad," he rumbled softly as he placed his fingers under the other gargoyle's chin. He ignored the smaller male's slight flinch and urged him to lift his gaze. Once Lionad's focus clashed with his own, Destrawn smiled and reminded, "Relax, Lionad. That's unnecessary here."

As Destrawn lowered his hand, he watched Lionad's shoulders relax. The other male nodded just a little as a hint of a smile danced around the corners of his lips. He even managed to continue holding Destrawn's gaze.

"Sorry, Destrawn," Lionad mumbled. "Sometimes . . . it's hard to remember."

Destrawn nodded. "I don't doubt it." Then, addressing the reason the gargoyle approached him in the first place, Destrawn indicated the buffet of food. "I'll snag a couple of breakfast burritos and be right there."

Lionad nodded. "I'll let Chieftain Kinsey know, Second." Then the other gargoyle hurried toward a nearby table.

As Destrawn resumed his journey to the buffet, he noticed Lionad stop beside a slender human. The expression of concern on the male's face immediately morphed into a smile as Lionad threaded a clawed hand through his hair. Then the gargoyle bent and kissed his mate before grabbing a mug from the table and heading out of the cafeteria.

Destrawn couldn't help the small smile that curved his lips as he grabbed a plate and set it on the bar running before the buffet. It was good to see what a few reassuring words could do to lower the tension of those in the clutch. While he would never consider himself the romantic or compassionate sort, he knew the value of a simple act of kindness.

To that end, Destrawn tried to rein in his dominance when necessary.

As Destrawn placed a couple of pre-made sausage, egg, cheese, and potato burritos on his plate, he sensed someone approach. His nose told him it was Rundin. As Destrawn added four egg, ham, and cheese croissant-wiches to his plate, he turned his head and nodded at the little gargoyle.

"Good morning, Second Destrawn," Rundin greeted with a shy smile.

Destrawn offered the much smaller gargoyle a slight smile in return. "Good morning, Rundin." After a second of hesitation, he forced himself to add, "I spotted you out on the patio after I woke from roost. You must have hustled out there as soon as you could."

Rundin scented of pleasure, as if he liked knowing Destrawn had noticed him. "Praerna told me how much work still needed to be done," he claimed, referring to another small, unmated gargoyle. "So as soon as I could move, I rushed out to help." Peering at Destrawn from beneath his lashes, Rundin stated, "The party is going to be so much fun. You're coming, aren't you?"

"I'll be there," Destrawn confirmed, although he didn't add that it was more because he knew Chieftain Kinsey would question him if he didn't show up.

"Great!" Rundin eased closer, reached up, and rested his white-clawed hand on Destrawn's upper arm. "How's your neck and shoulders? Can I help you in any way?"

Destrawn knew Rundin was offering a massage . . . and even more, judging by the scent of his attraction.

Yeah, time to nip this in the bud. I'm just not certain how.

Fortunately, Destrawn didn't have to decide right away since he had an out. "I'm fine, Rundin," he replied, which was true due to spending several extra minutes under his showerhead. *So much less stress this way.* "But thank you for the offer."

The scent of Rundin's disappointment filled the air.

Before Destrawn could come up with a way to extricate himself without being abrupt and seeming rude, Sethnos came to his rescue. "Evening, Rundin," the enforcer greeted before turning his attention to Destrawn. "You ready, Destrawn?"

Obviously, the enforcer had been asked to the meeting by

Chieftain Kinsey, too.

Destrawn lifted the full plate in one hand and his half-full mug of coffee with the other. "I am. Let's get to our meeting." Then he pasted a small smile to his lips and focused on Rundin, giving the gargoyle a nod. "Have fun helping Praerna. I hear the party will be great."

Without waiting for Rundin to respond, Destrawn headed out of the cafeteria with Sethnos beside him carrying his own plate and mug.

Once the door had closed behind them, Destrawn let out a deep breath. He shook his head a little. Upon hearing Sethnos's low chuckle, he sent a side-eyed look the enforcer's way.

Upon spotting Sethnos's amused smirk, Destrawn narrowed his eyes and growled, "What?"

Sethnos shrugged even as his smile grew wider. "Rundin has a thing for you."

Destrawn groaned softly, nodding. "I know." Frowning as he climbed the stairs and retraced his steps, returning to the wing that housed not only his own room, but those of the inner circle as well as Chieftain Kinsey's office. "I can't figure out why."

"You offered him a bit of kindness after he'd been repressed for decades," Sethnos guessed, arching one brow ridge as he eyed him. "I've never smelled your scents combined, so it's not sexual," he commented bluntly. "But Rundin sure wants it to be."

While Destrawn didn't often discuss his sex life with another, he realized Sethnos would be a safe one to do it with. "In my old clutch, I had a handful of sexual partners," he admitted. "No strings. Just the occasional use of each other's bodies for stress relief." *Huh. Maybe that's why I've been waking up tense these last couple of months.* Grimacing, Destrawn added, "I don't think Rundin would understand that arrangement."

"Definitely not," Sethnos replied, confirming Destrawn's assessment. "Even if you were to spell out that kind of arrangement with him"—he paused to open the door, and Destrawn preceded him into the chieftain's office—"I get the sense that as soon as he scents another on you, he'd freak out."

Destrawn nodded. "I'm certain you're right."

"Who are you talking about?" Chieftain Kinsey asked curiously from where he sat behind his desk.

Settling in the lounging area, Destrawn placed his plate and mug on the coffee table. "Rundin," he told his chieftain as he picked up one of the wrapped burritos.

Sethnos settled nearby, placing his mug on the end table between their chairs. Leaning backward, he opted to rest his plate on his thigh.

Chieftain Kinsey followed them and settled on the love seat. "You have a thing going on with Rundin?" He relaxed his arm along the back. "Is that wise?"

"Rundin needs a gentle and compassionate touch," a voice stated near the door, revealing that Kinsey's mate, Jimmy, had joined them from their attached sitting room suite. As Jimmy crossed to the chieftain, he eyed Destrawn curiously. "I mean, I know you can do gentle. I've seen it, but compassionate?" Cocking his head, a smile toyed around his lips as he sat beside Kinsey. "No offense, but you don't strike me as the most compassionate."

Placing his arm around Jimmy, Chieftain Kinsey tucked him against his side. "Fiercely loyal, dominant, and aggressive, yes." He chuckled as he shook his head. "Compassionate, no."

Having taken a big bite of his burrito, Destrawn nodded. "Not offended," he muttered around his mouthful of food. After swallowing, Destrawn added, "Which is why I need advice on how to help him get over his infatuation with me."

Snorting, he grumbled, "I'm definitely not boyfriend material."

Hell, Destrawn didn't even consider himself mate material. What did he know about taking care of someone's emotional needs? Physical needs, sure. But putting someone else's desires before his own? Not so much.

Yeah, I know I'm a selfish fucker.

"We'll give it some thought," Kinsey assured. Then a grin spread his lips. "While you're gone."

"Gone?" Narrowing his eyes, Destrawn asked, "Just where am I going, Kinsey?"

With only them in the room, Destrawn knew it was just fine to drop titles. Kinsey didn't stand on ceremony when it was just the inner circle. Destrawn liked that about him.

"I received a message from Master Krispin Stearling," Kinsey told him, lifting his mug to his lips. Before taking a sip, he revealed, "His trackers have discovered some troubling things regarding the activities of paranormal hunters, and he thinks it would be best if the report was shared in person."

Destrawn had been to Master Krispin's coven once before. The powerful vampire had ended up mated with one of their best trackers — Washington — when the gargoyle had followed a rogue there — Chasis. Their gargoyle clutch had worked with the coven to bring in Chasis, and they had a good working relationship with them.

Chowing on his breakfast, Destrawn didn't respond other than with a nod.

To Kinsey, that was enough. "Good. You'll leave as soon as you finish your breakfast."

Destrawn appreciated a reprieve from worrying about Rundin. With a nod, he took a sip of his coffee, then began eating faster.

CHAPTER TWO

Striding through the coven, Sorbin could only focus on one thing—reaching his shower. He'd had to use some unorthodox techniques to get the information his coven needed. Still, Sorbin had managed it, reaching a location where his enhanced vampire hearing could make out the conversation of a trio of humans he believed were paranormal hunters.

Sorbin had been right.

There had been two women and a man, and they were discussing the arrival time of not only a team of Priests, but how they were teaming up with a bunch of hunters.

None of it had been good news.

While Sorbin knew he needed to share everything with Master Krispin, he appreciated that his vampire leader understood his desire to clean up first. Krispin had set the time for the meeting in half an hour. It would be a quick shower, but that was okay. He desperately needed to get the scent of sewer off of him.

"Wooee!" Vicon called, waving a hand in front of his nose. The move didn't hide the huge grin on Sorbin's friend's face as he fell into step beside him. "What the hell have you been up to, Sorb?"

Rolling his eyes, Sorbin grumbled, "Just doing my job, Vic. You know how it is." Vicon worked as a guard, aiding in the security of the coven. "You've had to break up fights you would rather wish you hadn't."

"Ain't that the truth," Vicon replied with a nod. "That cheating asshole totally would have deserved that beat-down."

Sorbin almost reached out and patted his friend on the shoulder, but he stayed the action at the last second. He didn't want to get his buddy dirty. The man was dressed in a hotel security uniform, so was probably about to start his shift.

"Maybe the guy caught up with the cheater later," Sorbin offered in commiseration, knowing Vicon had a particular distaste for liars, and cheaters were the worst of the lot. "And he did break up with him."

Nodding, Vicon asked again, "So what happened to you?"

"Sewer," Sorbin answered simply. "It was the only way I could get close enough to where a few humans were meeting." With a waggle of his eyebrows and a wide grin, he claimed, "But it paid off."

"You always get what you need." Vicon lifted his hand, then froze. Grinning widely, he pointed at Sorbin instead. "My shift ends in four hours. If you're still here, we should meet at the bar and catch up."

Sorbin nodded. "If I'm here, absolutely," he agreed. "I'll text you, Donny, and Lathe," Sorbin added, referring to their other buddies.

Vicon gave him a thumbs up, then turned down another hallway.

Gratefully, Sorbin didn't run into anyone else on his way to his suite. He grabbed a plastic bag from under his kitchen sink before making his way to the bathroom. As Sorbin stripped, he placed each article in the sack, right down to his socks and underwear. Once naked, he tied the top shut.

Sorbin set the bag aside, intending to just throw the acrid clothes in the trash. They were easily replaced, after all. Hopping in the shower, Sorbin turned the water on as hot as he could handle and scrubbed . . . several times over.

Once Sorbin could no longer smell sewer sludge, he hopped out of the shower and dried off. A check of the time on his phone told him he had less than ten minutes. He rushed around his bedroom and closet, yanking on jeans, a comfortable polo, and a pair of sandals, since he hated putting socks and shoes on his wet feet.

As Sorbin strode swiftly from his suite, he finger-combed his wet, sandy-blond hair, pushing the shaggy locks away from his face and tucking some behind his ears. It wasn't ideal, but it was better than nothing. There was no way he wanted to keep his coven leaders waiting.

Reaching the conference room, Sorbin paused. He took a deep breath to steady his nerves. It didn't matter how many times he gave a report to his inner circle — he always felt a skitter of nerves under his skin.

Sorbin respected the hell out of Master Krispin, and he never wanted to disappoint him.

Except, this time, there was a subtle scent that distracted him. Cocking his head, he took another breath, then a third. His body warmed more than the hot shower had accomplished, and he even felt his blood simmer within his veins.

Huh. That's odd.

Shaking his head, Sorbin did his best to ignore the odd reaction as he lifted his hand and gripped the door handle. He turned it, pushed it open, and headed inside. As soon as Sorbin entered, that same scent intensified, causing him to pause.

"Ah, Sorbin. Excellent," Master Krispin called in lieu of a greeting. "Glad you've arrived. Come in."

Sorbin yanked his attention to Master Krispin and did as he'd been bidden. Closing the door behind him, he took a second to peer around the room. He recognized almost everyone . . . except the huge gargoyle sitting on a love seat and taking up nearly the entire thing.

Unable to help himself, Sorbin found his gaze riveted to the striking male. He'd met his master's beloved — a slender, medium-brown-hided gargoyle named Wash. This one, though . . . was quite different.

The male's hide was a dark-green hue, which set off the massive black wings draped over his shoulders perfectly. The way the gargoyle had pulled his black hair away from his face in some kind of tail accentuated his square jaw. The gargoyle's shoulders were broad, and what Sorbin could see of his seated frame appeared heavily muscled.

"This is Second Destrawn, of the Aerasceatle clutch."

Sorbin knew it was Master Krispin speaking, but he couldn't seem to tear his gaze away from the gargoyle.

"Due to the little you told me, I felt a representative of Chieftain Kinsey's should be on hand." The master's voice grew a bit sharper. "Sorbin?"

Finally, Sorbin yanked his attention from the gorgeous specimen of maleness. "Yes, Master." He forced his feet to move, striding deeper into the room. "Uh, my apologies." Unable to help himself, Sorbin flicked his gaze to Second Destrawn. He cleared his throat before managing to add, "Nice to meet you, Second."

As Sorbin moved closer, the scent he'd noticed outside the door intensified. His mouth began to water, and even his fangs tingled. He swallowed hard, as once again, he froze.

"Holy shit," Sorbin mumbled as a suspicion formed.

Destrawn's thick eyebrow ridges drew together as he narrowed his eyes. Tipping up his chin, he flared his nostrils as he inhaled deeply. He blinked as confusion filled his features.

To Sorbin's surprise, Destrawn parted his lips and flicked out his tongue. He pulled the appendage back into his mouth and snapped it shut. A shell-shocked expression crossed his face as he swallowed so hard his Adam's apple bobbed.

"That is . . . unexpected," Destrawn rumbled, his deep voice causing the hairs on Sorbin's arms to stand on end.

Sorbin knew what he suspected, and it seemed that same possibility had just hit Destrawn. Unfortunately, the gargoyle didn't appear excited. Instead, Destrawn looked . . . concerned.

"Second Destrawn?" Master Krispin cut in. "Is everything okay?"

Destrawn blinked, then panned his focus slowly left until he stared at Krispin. "That remains to be seen, Master Krispin."

"What do you mean?" Second Ridger asked, leaning forward in his seat. The second of the vampire coven cradled his tumbler between his palms as he glanced between everyone. "What's going on?"

"We may have a . . . complication," Destrawn rumbled as he rose to his feet. Lifting his wings from his shoulders, he allowed them to billow behind him as he stalked toward Sorbin. Destrawn trapped Sorbin's focus in an intense gaze, his gray eyes dark like storm clouds. "But we should know for certain, shouldn't we, Tracker Sorbin?"

Sorbin felt rooted to where he stood as he nodded slowly. As Destrawn drew closer, he tipped his head back as he looked up . . . and up. The male was tall, topping Sorbin's own height of six-foot-one by over half a foot. Since Destrawn had lifted his wings, Sorbin could see exactly how big and broad he was. The firm tilt of his lips and the way he narrowed his eyes caused his gut to clench, arousal swimming through his veins.

"Hmmm." Destrawn stopped before him. He bent a little and nuzzled against Sorbin's temple, encouraging him to tilt his neck. "There's something about your scent," Destrawn muttered. "Something that's throwing me off."

For a second, Sorbin could do little but pant as he enjoyed the feel of the large gargoyle's light touches. Then what the male actually said registered. He also recalled something else unique to gargoyles.

They had the best sense of smell of any paranormal—far

more sensitive than a vampire's.

Feeling his cheeks heat, Sorbin fought down a wave of embarrassment. "Uh, I had to hide out in a sewer to get the information we needed."

Destrawn straightened, nodding. "Ah, that would explain it." The corners of his lips quirked up in a smile that held a hint of arrogance. "I can smell the fresh soap on you, but I'll wash you again."

Sorbin felt the hairs on his neck stand on end, and he frowned. "I can wash myself," he grumbled. Narrowing his eyes as he stared at Destrawn, he declared, "The only reason you can smell it is because you're a gargoyle."

I sure hope that's the truth.

Destrawn shrugged one massive shoulder negligently. "The point is, I *can* smell it, and I don't like it."

As Sorbin opened his mouth to reply, Destrawn lifted his hands and used the fore-claw of his left hand to slice into the wrist of his right. His blood pooled from between the broken skin, flooding the room with its exquisite aroma. Sorbin fought back a moan as he snapped his mouth closed so he could lick his lips.

Lifting his wrist close to Sorbin's face, Destrawn purred, "Taste me."

Sorbin stared at the delicious-smelling blood pooling on Destrawn's wrist. Licking his lips, he tore his gaze away from it and focused on the gargoyle's face. The male's narrowed gaze screamed dominance and . . . superiority.

Am I misreading him?

"Drink, Sorbin," Destrawn ordered again. "I don't want to have to cut myself a second time."

Nope. Not misreading him.

Even as Sorbin wondered why Fate would pair him with someone like Destrawn, he knew he didn't have a choice. Rejecting the male would do no good. Once a vampire scented their fated beloved, their ability to feed from others would begin to wane.

Lifting one hand, Sorbin gripped Destrawn's thick wrist just below where he'd cut himself. He noticed the way the gargoyle narrowed his eyes in his peripheral vision. When Sorbin slipped out his tongue and swiped it over Destrawn's torn flesh, he scooped up a large dollop of the gargoyle's life-giving fluid.

The rich flavor of Destrawn's blood flowed across Sorbin's taste buds. His mouth watered for more, and he couldn't resist licking the gargoyle's wrist again. He felt his fangs tingle, and he fought his need to sink them deep into Destrawn, penetrating his hide.

Destrawn's low growl caught Sorbin's attention.

Peering up through his lashes, Sorbin took in Destrawn's expression. He saw his flared nostrils and how he'd parted his lips. His deep gray eyes had somehow managed to darken even further, and there was even a hint of a flush on his dark cheeks.

When Destrawn rested his free hand on the back of Sorbin's neck and tightened his grip, Sorbin realized he was still suckling on the gargoyle's flesh.

Even though Sorbin longed to drink properly from his beloved, the sound of a throat clearing reminded him of where he was.

Right. Audience.

As Sorbin lifted his mouth free of Destrawn's wrist, he wiped the back of his mouth with his hand. At the same time, he leveled a hard stare at the gargoyle.

"You never need to cut yourself to feed me blood, Destrawn," Sorbin stated flatly. "I'm a vampire, remember?" He grinned, but he knew it wasn't a friendly look as ire continued to fill him, regardless of the fact that he'd just found his beloved. "And you injured, for any reason, is not acceptable."

Destrawn's nostrils flared, and his eyes narrowed. "Of

course, Sorbin," he replied gruffly. "I'll do my best to remember that." Lifting his hand from Sorbin's neck, Destrawn moved it to Sorbin's wrist. He used the hold to loosen Sorbin's grip. Then he threaded his fingers through Sorbin's so they were holding hands. "Come."

Sorbin found himself being tugged toward the small sofa Destrawn had been sitting on. Glancing Master Krispin's way, he saw the amused tilt of his lips. The master was exchanging glances with Second Ridger and Head Enforcer Basques.

Upon reaching the sofa, Sorbin worried Destrawn would expect him to sit on his lap. After all, the gargoyle had pretty much been taking up the entire space.

That so will not be happening.

Fortunately, Destrawn sat a little more to the side. "Sit beside me, my mate," he ordered with a tug of their joined hands.

There wasn't a whole lot of room, but Sorbin was a slender vampire. He could make it work. The alternative was unthinkable.

Sorbin eased onto the sofa, doing his best to keep a little space between himself and Destrawn. The gargoyle didn't allow that, however. Destrawn wrapped his arm around him, as well as a wing, and tucked Sorbin into his side.

Destrawn stared down at Sorbin for a few seconds, and his eyes narrowed as if he knew exactly what he'd been trying to do—keep distance between them.

Then Destrawn turned his attention to Master Krispin. "Yes, we have a complication," he declared. "Because if we're going up against humans after paranormals, there's no way my mate is getting anywhere near them."

Gaping, Sorbin stared in shock upon hearing Destrawn's heavy-handed declaration. Then he growled and shook his head.

No fucking way.

"You just wait one damn minute, Destrawn," Sorbin snarled, glaring at the gargoyle who regarded him stoically. "That's not a choice you can make. I'm the one who found these assholes. That means I'm part of this." Pointing at Destrawn, Sorbin claimed, "And that means I'm helping get rid of them."

CHAPTER THREE

Destrawn fought back a stab of annoyance upon hearing Sorbin's claim. Opening his mouth, he readied to reiterate that his mate would in no way put himself in danger. Just the idea of Sorbin anywhere near those who hunted paranormals caused his blood to chill.

It also helped get his raging hard-on under control.

Being in a room full of paranormals, Destrawn wasn't embarrassed in the least to be sporting an erection behind his loincloth. Every man in the room knew how a paranormal would be affected by meeting one's mate. Getting a boner was a natural and healthy response.

"That's something the pair of you can discuss in private," Master Krispin cut in, raising his hand to further catch their attention. "First, we need to hear Sorbin's report in regards to the humans after us."

Destrawn clenched his jaw, fighting his desire to counter the vampire master. His mate had refused his order. He needed to get it through his newly found vampire that his life in danger simply wasn't acceptable.

Shouldn't Sorbin have understood that instinctually?

On instinct, Destrawn tightened not only the arm he had around Sorbin but his wing as well. Maybe if he kept his mate close to his side, he could keep him out of danger. Except, that wouldn't work, since Destrawn had to be on the front line to stop these bastards from hurting anyone in his clutch.

"Good," Master Krispin stated, having misunderstood Destrawn's silence.

Oh, well. Later.

Master Krispin relaxed back on his love seat. Resting his whiskey tumbler on the arm, he tapped the crystal glass with his forefinger. He placed his left hand on Wash's thigh where his gargoyle mate sat beside him.

"Now then," the vampire master began, looking relaxed and comfortable. "Please share everything you've found, Sorbin. Leave no detail out, regardless of how trivial it may seem."

"Of course, Master Krispin," Sorbin replied.

When Sorbin attempted to straighten in his seat, essentially pulling away from him, Destrawn tightened his hold.

Sorbin growled softly as he frowned at Destrawn. "I'm not about to go zipping off to find the nearest paranormal hunter if you allow me to sit up straight," he stated, his tone rough. The scent of his vampire's ire filled the air.

Shit. Why does mating have to be so hard? What the hell was Fate thinking? I don't have what it takes to be a good mate.

Ten minutes with Sorbin had made that painfully obvious already.

Fighting his natural instinct to keep his newly found mate close—one that smelled off because of where he'd been traveling, making Destrawn want to replace the smell with his own in the worst way—he relaxed his hold.

Straightening, Sorbin rubbed his free palm over his thigh. To Destrawn's relief, he didn't try to pull his other free of his grip. Knowing he had to express something other than his bullheaded dominance, he squeezed the vampire's hand lightly, hoping to convey his pleasure.

Sorbin glanced Destrawn's way for an instant, questions in his pale blue eyes.

Destrawn forced what he hoped was a grateful smile. When Sorbin's eyebrows furrowed and he returned his attention back to the vampire inner circle, he wasn't certain if he'd pulled it off. Still, his mate wasn't pulling away, so he would worry about it later.

"As you directed, Master Krispin, Merlick and I" — Sorbin paused and focused on Destrawn — "he's another tracker in the coven" — then he returned his focus to the master — "have been following leads given to us by Belial and Gabriel." Once again, Sorbin focused on Destrawn. "Gabriel is a vampire from a nearby coven in Montana, and Belial is his demon beloved."

Destrawn lifted his free hand and touched Sorbin's forearm. "No need to explain all the players, my mate," he stated. "Master Krispin has shared a number of reports with Chieftain Kinsey, and I have been privy to their information." Doing his best to keep any hint of condescension or impatience from his tone, Destrawn told his mate, "I know who all the players on our side are."

Sorbin nodded once, then resumed his explanations. "You remember the woman Tiffany met with a week prior to her" — Sorbin grinned — "meltdown due to stress?"

Krispin smirked. "Of course."

Due to having read those aforementioned reports, Destrawn knew that Tiffany was the ex-mayor Tiffany Bickerman. She'd been one of the one percent of humans who hadn't been influenced by a vampire's trancing abilities, and she'd somehow learned about vampires. She'd discovered that Krispin was one and had wanted him to marry her and extend her life so they could rule the city together.

Talk about delusions of grandeur.

Krispin and his people had contacted another coven for aid, and the demon Belial had arrived, sent by the Horseman of War, to delve into her mind.

"Tiffany only had an alias for the woman, but Ninevah discovered her real name. Rebeccah Olsen." Sorbin grinned, clearly pleased with himself. "It was only a matter of tailing her after that. While sitting in a tavern, I overheard Rebeccah tell her companion that they'd be meeting Lady Milligan this afternoon at three in a park. The area was pretty open without any way for me to get close enough to overhear them." Grimacing, Sorbin explained, "Fortunately, I discovered the sewer tunnels the park had been built over." He rubbed the back of his neck as he cast an uneasy glance Destrawn's way. "Uh, I scrubbed, but—"

"I shouldn't have commented on your scent the way I did," Destrawn stated, cutting into Sorbin's apology. "I was . . . confused."

As Sorbin nodded, he looked back at the other vampires. "According to Rebeccah, a group of Priests will arrive at the warehouse on Benson at ten tomorrow night." Even as growls of anger rolled through the place, Sorbin scratched at his scalp and grimaced. "And that's not all."

Seeing the way Sorbin cast a wary glance his way, Destrawn scowled. "What is it?" Upon scenting his mate's rising unease, the bitter scent of fear filling his nostrils, a low growl rolled up his throat. Destrawn tightened his hold on Sorbin's hand. "Please tell me what concerns you, my mate. I will fix it."

Damn. These mating instincts kick in fast.

Sorbin cleared his expression, then met his gaze. "Lady Milligan is a hunter. A group of them are supposed to be moving into Lake Point at the same time," he stated levelly. "Somehow, they know about us both, and they're going to work together to coordinate an attack."

Destrawn let out a low, angry snarl. "When?" he demanded.

"New Year's Eve."

"Damn it," Destrawn roared, tightening his grip.

When Destrawn felt Sorbin flinch in his hold, he frowned at the vampire. Seeing his mate's bowed head and tense shoulders, Destrawn tried to figure out what the hell that was about. Then it hit him. Massaging Sorbin's pulse point with his thumb, Destrawn began to trill for his mate.

22

"I'm not a *shoot the messenger* type of guy, Sorbin," Destrawn claimed, nuzzling his temple. "I'm loud, dominant, controlling, and brash, but I'm not impulsive or violent." Feeling Sorbin begin to relax, he took it a step further, trusting in the whole fated mates thing. Destrawn licked at his vampire's temple, enjoying the man's flavor, before murmuring, "Besides, you're my mate, Sorbin. Sure, I can be a controlling son-of-a-bitch, and I often demand before asking, but you're still my mate. That means you're one of the only people in the world that can tell me off for it."

Sorbin's pale blue eyes widened. For a few seconds, he just stared.

Destrawn waited.

Finally, Sorbin's eyes narrowed. "That's not the impression I received after our first conversation twenty minutes ago."

Figuring he deserved that, he nodded. "Well, I'm still reeling from shock here. I didn't expect to meet my mate" — pausing, he grimaced, but he knew he needed to tell the vampire the truth — "for a good long while, yet. At least, well after things had settled in my new clutch."

"New clutch?"

Hearing the curiosity in Sorbin's tone, Destrawn nodded. "Yeah. I've only been there a little over a year. Most of the inner circle is new." He didn't really know how to explain his thoughts, which led him to blurt out, "I didn't move out here to find a mate. I came to . . . help right a wrong. Use my controlling nature to bring order to a disorganized clutch." Scratching at the tip of an ear with his left hand, Destrawn quickly added, "Under Chieftain Kinsey's guidance, of course."

No way did Destrawn want word to get back to his chieftain that he wanted to lead. That wasn't the case. While Destrawn loved control, he didn't need to be the big dog if he respected the gargoyle he answered to, and Kinsey made an exceptional chieftain.

"As much as I hate to break up the moment," Master Krispin stated, interrupting them. "We do need to make a call to Chieftain Kinsey . . . for several reasons."

Destrawn took a couple of seconds to continue staring at Sorbin. He was a gorgeous man, after all. His clear blue eyes called to Destrawn in a way he'd never experienced. The vampire's leanly muscled body begged for him to rake his claws lightly over his flesh. He wanted to —

Sorbin chuckled softly, a twinkle entering his eyes. "I like you looking at me like that better than when you offered me your blood."

Scoffing ever-so-softly, Destrawn nodded once. "Not my finest moment." Then he had to add, "Which I'll explain another time."

"Fair enough." Sorbin straightened once more and focused on Master Krispin. "Do you think it's safe to share this over the phone?"

Destrawn wondered the same thing, seeing as the last he'd heard, he'd been sent because they weren't certain their lines were secure.

Krispin nodded. "I received word from Ninevah fifteen minutes before the conference that he's put together a secure line for us." He pulled his phone free and began dialing.

As Krispin did that, Destrawn lifted his glass of spiced rum from the end table and took a sip. Recalling that his mate hadn't been given a drink upon entering — mostly due to the shock of them discovering their connection — he offered it to Sorbin. "Would you like a drink?"

Sorbin took the tumbler and sniffed it. With a hum, he took a large swallow. Licking his lips, he handed it back. "Thanks."

Destrawn finished the glass, chuckling as he set it aside. "Guess we're gonna need a refill on that," he stated with a wink.

"Master Krispin." Chieftain Kinsey's deep voice filled the room, coming from the speaker on the vampire master's phone. "How is the meeting going? Is everything okay?"

Krispin hummed as a smile toyed at the edges of his lips. "Yes and no," he replied.

Kinsey growled softly. "You know I don't have a tech guy, yet, so will you tell me if the line is secure?"

"It's secure, Kinsey," Krispin assured, dropping formality. "And I'll have a guy assist you with that until you get a gargoyle trained."

"Who's in the room, Kris?" Kinsey also dropped formality.

"My inner circle. My beloved. Destrawn is also here." Krispin smiled in their direction. "As well as my tracker, Sorbin."

"How was your trip, Destrawn?" Kinsey asked, probably more as a way to confirm he was there and being treated well.

Destrawn replied, "Smooth and uneventful. I love a good night flight." Before his chieftain could ask more, he added, "And when Krispin said yes and no, he meant that we have good news and bad news."

Kinsey groaned. "What else is new," he grumbled, which pulled a smirk to Destrawn's lips. After a drawn-out sigh from his chieftain, he ordered, "Okay. Bad news first."

"Hunters are gathering in Lake Point." Destrawn saw no reason to sugar coat it. Even as Kinsey's growl came through the line, he continued, "That's not the worst of it."

"Of course, it's not," Kinsey grumbled. "What is it?"

"They intend to attack New Year's Eve . . . the day of our party."

"What the hell?" Kinsey bellowed. "How the fuck could they know about our party?"

"I doubt they do," Sorbin cut in, attempting to rise.

Destrawn could read his need to move by the twitch of his hand within his own. Rising, too, he urged his mate to his feet. Sorbin actually smiled at him gratefully.

Then Destrawn released Sorbin, telling him, "I'll get us both a drink. Tell our chieftain what you found out and what you mean."

"Our chieftain?" Sorbin muttered, frowning. "What do you mean?"

Chuckling, Destrawn pointed toward the phone as he grabbed his empty tumbler. "I bet you think New Year's Eve is a coincidence."

"Well, sure," Sorbin replied immediately. "No way would hunters think that monsters would celebrate a human holiday." Grimacing, the vampire quickly added, "No offense."

Destrawn snorted as he crossed to the sideboard and helped himself. "Oh, no offense taken, Sorbin," he told his vampire. *Damn, I'm definitely warming up to the idea of the vampire being mine.* "We know that hunters think of us as monsters." Lifting one shoulder while pulling out another tumbler, Destrawn rolled his eyes as he poured more spiced rum into both of them. "Monsters. Beasts. A form of demon that uses a familiar to bind us to this plane." He pointed at Sorbin. "Someone we call a mate."

Sorbin nodded. "Right." Then the vampire cleared his throat. "So, I know it's New Year's Eve because of Lady Milligan's comment," he explained, moving restlessly around the perimeter of the room. "She said all the groups were coming together for a last-ditch effort, a last *push*, to ensure as few abominations make it into the new year as possible."

While Sorbin took the tumbler Destrawn held out to him, Kinsey let out an annoyed growl. "Got it. I'll send scouts into the town. We have a few contacts there." A second later, he asked, "Destrawn, what did you mean by *our* chieftain? Are you talking about Wash, because really, his loyalties sort of lie with Krispin now."

Even as Wash began softly chuckling, Destrawn couldn't help but grin. "Well, as it turns out, that's the good news,

Chieftain." For some reason, unable to wait to share his good—if unexpected—fortune, Destrawn quickly stated, "Sorbin is my mate."

For a second, silence hung in the air.

Then, to Destrawn's surprise, Kinsey barked a laugh. "Congratulations, Destrawn. You could use someone to mellow you . . . and of course, that will get Rundin off your back." Before Destrawn could think up a response to that, Kinsey continued, barking, "Ha! Take that, Krispin! I *told* you the next one was mine."

Destrawn saw the surprise on Sorbin's face, which mirrored how he felt. Arching one brow ridge, he focused on the vampire master.

Krispin chuckled softly as he shook his head, all the while pinning his gaze on Sorbin. "Just like your gargoyles here are always part of your clutch, Sorbin will always remain part of my coven."

Before Sorbin could voice the questions in his beautiful blue eyes, Destrawn asked, "What are you guys talking about?"

The vampire master smirked. "After Dloben and Wash came to live here with their vampires, Kinsey claimed the next pairing between our groups had to go there." His expression sobered a little as he focused on Sorbin. "Guess he was right."

"Go *there*?" Sorbin questioned.

Destrawn realized they had so much to talk about.

CHAPTER FOUR

Sorbin glanced at where Destrawn stood beside his bed. His body thrummed with arousal, and his mouth watered with his desire to taste the gargoyle's blood once more. He wanted to lay his beloved down and trace every inch of his wings.

After the meeting had ended, Sorbin had followed Master Krispin's advice and had taken Destrawn to his suite. That way they could talk—being alone and near a bed was damn distracting, though.

From having a couple of other gargoyles join their coven, Sorbin had heard the rumors. Gargoyles with male mates traditionally topped and bottomed, so they could go through molt—the process that gave them a human form. Except, looking at Destrawn's crossed arms and intense expression, Sorbin didn't get the impression that he would be willing.

Since a gargoyle couldn't bottom for a female mate, Sorbin figured there had to be another way, too.

If Destrawn isn't willing, I know our sex life is going to end up . . . unfulfilling.

While Sorbin enjoyed being on the receiving end, he was a switch. He liked both positions, and in the couple of friends-with-benefits relationships he'd been in, positions hadn't been exclusive. It had been one of Sorbin's requirements.

And another thing—

"I can't just pick up and leave," Sorbin claimed, rubbing his hand through his hair. "My family is here. Friends. I—"

"You have family here?" Destrawn cut in. "Parents? Siblings?" Before Sorbin could answer, Destrawn pointed out,

"It's common for family to shift between covens due to our life spans." Destrawn lowered his arms and began stalking toward Sorbin. "It is the way of paranormals. We meet our mate and choose which clutch or coven or pack we should live at."

"And so that automatically means your clutch?" Sorbin pressed. It was his turn to plant his feet and cross his arms. "Dloben and Wash are here."

Destrawn's thick lips curved a bit in an obviously amused smirk. "Of course, they are, because them moving here made sense."

The gargoyle rested his big hands on Sorbin's shoulders, and Sorbin could feel the heat through his thin polo shirt. Even as Sorbin wished the gargoyle would remove his shirt so he could feel those clawed fingers on his flesh, his beloved kept talking, helping him stay focused.

"Dloben is mated with your coven's head enforcer," Destrawn reminded him. He massaged Sorbin's shoulders gently. His gray eyes glimmered with a hungry gleam in the bedroom light, betraying his need as he swept his gaze over Sorbin's frame. "And Wash mated with your vampire master. It makes sense for them to move here." Sliding his hand up, Destrawn scraped his claws lightly over the skin of his neck, sending goose bumps down Sorbin's arms, until he cradled his jaw. Then he rubbed his thumb-claw under Sorbin's lip, making it difficult to concentrate as the gargoyle stated, "And I am the second of my clutch. Just as your inner circle leaders could not leave their coven, I cannot leave my clutch. I need you to move there, my mate. Will you do it?"

Sorbin fought back a tremble as his body ignited from the sensual touches. Unable to fight off his own need to touch, he brought his hands up and rested them on either side of Destrawn's ribcage. The swarthy hide under his palms felt different than anything he'd experienced before, and he couldn't resist rubbing his hands up a little, then back down, tracing along the gargoyle's deep green skin.

"What family are you worried about leaving behind, Sorbin?"

When Destrawn asked that, Sorbin realized his brain had checked out, and he hadn't answered the male's prior question. He had asked—actually *asked*, not demanded or assumed as he'd done back in the conference room—if Sorbin would move to his clutch. He did his best to bank his arousal because they had a few things to talk about.

"Not a brother by blood," Sorbin admitted. "But one by bond. His name is Lathe."

Destrawn bent and nuzzled Sorbin's temple with his cheek, then licked over the flesh there. "Invite him to come live with us," he purred into his ear. "There's room."

Sorbin couldn't stop the shiver that racked his body. The hairs on his neck stood on end. His blood fired in his veins, and he gripped Destrawn's torso tighter as his knees threatened to go weak.

Holy shit!

Unable to recall ever reacting to another with even a small percentage of the need swirling through him, Sorbin fought against the pull to give in, to say—*to hell with it*—and begin bonding.

Gritting his teeth, Sorbin turned his head and met Destrawn's feral gaze. "I can ask, but are you sure you can give permission?"

In fact, he was damn sure Lathe wouldn't want to stick around even with Vicon and Donny still there. Thinking of them, he knew he would miss his buddies. Still, for his mate, he knew he had to make concessions, and Destrawn was right about who needed to move.

Destrawn chuckled, sending warm breath over his skin. "Oh, yes, my mate. As clutch second, I can give permission," he assured, sliding his thumb over Sorbin's lower lip. "I'm getting very impatient to taste these," he rumbled, beginning to lower his head. "Tell me yes. Tell me we can begin. I know my blood calls to you."

"It does," Sorbin murmured, seeing no need to deny what Destrawn's senses would be able to tell him. That didn't stop him from adding, "There is still one more thing to discuss."

Growling softly, Destrawn slid his left hand from Sorbin's shoulder down to his ass. "What now?" he demanded, right before he used his grip to lift Sorbin.

Sorbin would forever deny the squeak of surprise. He flailed for a second before wrapping his arms around the big gargoyle's neck. Before he could even fathom what his beloved intended, Sorbin was whirled in the air, and he felt his back land on the comforter.

Destrawn's big body pressed him into the mattress as he followed him down. Bracing his weight on his forearms, he used his knees to spread Sorbin's thighs. His dark eyes bore into him as he pinned him under his much larger body.

The male's huge black wings were spread behind him, perhaps for balance, and Sorbin found his gaze drawn to them. He still wanted to pet them, so he gave in to the urge.

Reaching beyond Destrawn, Sorbin skimmed his fingertips up the top ridgeline. The hard bone felt covered in velvety softness. Enjoying the smoothness under his fingers, Sorbin skimmed down the billowing appendage a little, as much as he could, before moving back to the top.

"S-Sorbin."

Hearing the way Destrawn rumbled his name, filled with a mixture of arousal and pleasure, Sorbin snapped his gaze to the gargoyle's face. He sucked in a surprised breath upon seeing the pleasure-pain expression etched across his features. Unable to resist, Sorbin repeated his gentle petting.

Destrawn's lips parted, and his breaths came in ragged pants. His chest heaved, and a low moan rumbled from him.

His eyes became heavy-lidded, and his pupils dilated. Even the scent of his arousal intensified.

"Damn, Dee," Sorbin muttered. "Are your wings . . . an erogenous zone?"

After swallowing so hard his Adam's apple bobbed, Destrawn met his gaze. "Yessss," he hissed before another groan ripped from him. "Heard it was but didn't realize—" Another moan coupled with a shudder cut off Destrawn's words.

Smug satisfaction flooded Sorbin at what Destrawn's broken words insinuated. Plus, the way his wings fluttered under his touch, bringing them closer to his fingers, then farther away, told Sorbin of his beloved's tortured enjoyment. He intended to capitalize on that as often as he needed to bring the clearly dominant gargoyle to heel.

A little persuasion never hurt anyone.

With that idea in mind, Sorbin brought one hand to Destrawn's jaw as he continued to fondle the section of wing he could reach over the big male's shoulder. "Tell me something, Dee," Sorbin crooned, brushing his fingertips along the ends of his pointed ear. "Any other zones I should know about? Places I should play with as I slide my cock into your ass, over and over."

As Sorbin had figured, after one heartbeat, two, Destrawn reached up and grabbed his wrists. He moved Sorbin's hands to either side of his head, then threaded their fingers together. With furrowed eyebrow ridges, he breathed deeply a few times, obviously trying to get himself under control.

Finally, Destrawn blinked and appeared to truly focus on him. "Um, about that . . ."

Sorbin narrowed his eyes and stated, "Don't tell me you're an exclusive top." When Destrawn's gaze slid to his left and uncertainty filled his eyes, Sorbin lifted his head and whispered into his ear, "Because I'm a switch, Destrawn. I like to bottom, but I enjoy sliding my dick into a lover, too."

Growling, the sound low and angry, Destrawn snapped his gaze back to Sorbin. He glared as he declared, "Do not speak to me of past lovers, Sorbin." Destrawn's grip on his fingers tightened. "You're mine."

"Yes, I am," Sorbin confirmed, because what was the point of denying it? Now that he'd met his beloved, there was no going back. "And you're mine. That means working out our differences."

Although Sorbin had no desire to think about his beloved with others, it was foolish to think otherwise. After all, he had no idea how old the gargoyle was. Due to that, he needed a little more information.

"Have you ever bottomed, Destrawn?" Sorbin asked, deciding to be blunt.

Groaning under his breath, Destrawn muttered, "Do we have to discuss this now?" His feral gaze bore into Sorbin's eyes. "Because I'd much rather be fucking you."

Sorbin didn't really want to talk, either. His dick ached, and it took every bit of self-control he possessed to keep from rocking his hips, from grinding his throbbing hard-on against the big male pressing against him. Still, one of them had to focus.

"I want you to fuck me, too," Sorbin began.

That seemed to be enough for Destrawn. The gargoyle released his hands. He grabbed the fabric of his polo shirt, but instead of pulling it over his head, he dug in his claws. The sound of rending fabric filled the room as Destrawn shredded his shirt.

Sorbin gasped at the unexpected move, and his dick jerked within the confines of his jeans. He groaned as Destrawn rocked back onto his calves, removing the chance for stimulus on his cock. Then he spotted his beloved hooking his claws into the waistband of his jeans, and his lust cleared . . . just a little.

"Stop," Sorbin gasped. He grabbed Destrawn's wrists. "I like these jeans."

"Then you better kick those off damn fast," Destrawn ordered, lifting his hands. He moved them to the ties holding his loincloth in place. With a quick, practiced-looking move, Destrawn stripped the bit of fabric, revealing his thick, around ten-inch, dark-green erection. Dropping the loincloth over the side of the bed with one hand, Destrawn gripped his length with the other. "I need inside you, mate."

An appreciative moan ripped from Sorbin's throat. He undid his fly and quickly shimmied out of his jeans, tossing them aside, kicking off his sandals in the process. As Sorbin reached over and grabbed the lube from his nightstand, he knew not everything was resolved, but he couldn't help the need burning through his body.

Sorbin needed the edge off, and it seemed that Destrawn decided to do that by fucking him.

As soon as Destrawn spotted the lube in his hand, a feral grin curved his lips. He wrapped his big hands around Sorbin's hips and used the hold to flip him. As soon as Sorbin's stomach hit the comforter, Destrawn sprawled over him.

"Mmm." Destrawn nuzzled the back of his neck, licking and nipping. "Gonna make you smell like me."

Feeling Destrawn's thick rod riding his cleft, Sorbin couldn't help but tense. He hadn't been on the receiving end in a good six months, and his beloved was packing a monster. Sorbin knew he would need plenty of prep.

"Relax, my mate," Destrawn rumbled, having obviously felt Sorbin tense. He ran his right hand down his side, lightly scraping his claws. "I'll take ever-so-good care of you." After pecking a kiss to the flesh where Sorbin's neck met his shoulder, Destrawn took the tube of lube from him. "I'm going to make you fly."

Sorbin turned his head to peer over his shoulder at Destrawn when his beloved lifted, putting a bit of space between their bodies. As much as he knew it was necessary, he suddenly wanted to call the gargoyle back. The air on his hot back caused goose bumps to break out on his flesh.

"After this, we're gonna talk," Sorbin declared. When Destrawn lifted his focus from where he was pouring slick onto his fingers, Sorbin gave him a firm look. "Aren't we?"

Destrawn licked his bottom lip, then nodded once. "We will. You are my mate. You deserve" — he blew out a harsh breath — "the truth."

For a second, Sorbin wanted to ask right then and there. Whatever it was, his beloved's shoulders tensed just thinking about it. Then Destrawn tossed the lube aside and rested one hand on his hip, teasing his claws over the soft skin of his groin, distracting him.

"Lift your hips, Sorbin," Destrawn ordered. "Present for your mate."

Sorbin bit back a moan at the image that popped into his head upon hearing Destrawn's words. As he eased onto his knees, keeping his weight on his forearms, and arched his back, he thought of his beloved in the same position. He knew nothing would be as gorgeous as that.

I could slide one hand all over his wings, distracting him, as I sink the fingers of my other hand into his chute. I'll tease his ring, massage his inner walls, and play with his prostate. His moans will be music to my ears, and I'll —

"Are you still with me, my mate?" Destrawn murmured while sliding his slicked fingers up and down his trench. As he massaged Sorbin's opening, he added, "Tell me where you went."

Unable to lie to his beloved, Sorbin twisted a little and held Destrawn's gaze. "I was thinking about what it would feel like to play with your wings as I open you up. I loved the feel of them, and how you responded to my touch was out of this world sexy."

Destrawn's features tightened for just an instant before he seemed to get control of himself. Then a small smile curved the corners of his lips. He dipped his head in a nod.

"We'll get to that," Destrawn told him. "Promise."

Taking his beloved at his word, Sorbin smiled. "Take me, Destrawn." He rocked his ass a little, pushing into the gargoyle's light touches. "Start the bonding process."

With a growl, Destrawn needed no further encouragement. He pressed his finger harder against his guardian muscle. Sorbin pushed out, and in the next instant, he felt his new and forever lover's thick digit slide into his body.

Destrawn growled into his ear as with unerring accuracy, he pegged Sorbin's pleasure gland.

Sparks of pleasure erupted through Sorbin's body, and he cried out his delight.

Oh, yeah.

CHAPTER FIVE

Destrawn's heart thudded wildly in his chest. His blood raged through his veins. He barely managed to keep from blowing his load upon feeling the tight squeeze to his finger.

My mate is so damn tight.

While Destrawn would never ask Sorbin how long it'd been since he'd been on the receiving end, he knew it had to have been a while. His mate's channel would take a bit of work to stretch him enough to accommodate his thickness. Destrawn never wanted to cause his mate a second of pain, but he feared he wouldn't be able to wait long enough to get it done.

"Another, Dee," Sorbin encouraged, rocking his hips up. "I can take it." A growl entered his voice as he added, "I'm a vampire. I'm not frail. Give us what we both need."

Then Sorbin clenched his chute around Destrawn's embedded digit.

Destrawn groaned at the sensation. His cock jerked at his groin, eager to replace his finger. Obeying his mate, he eased his finger mostly free, then pushed it back in again.

After two more passes, where Destrawn teased over Sorbin's prostate each time, he carefully sank in a second finger. To his relief, he heard Sorbin's hum of pleasure. His mate's heady scent of arousal and desire continued to flood the room. He even continued to rock into each of his moves.

Unable to help himself, Destrawn quickly eased in a third finger. When Sorbin immediately tensed up, he sucked at where his shoulder met his neck. At the same time, he moved just the tips of his fingers to tease over Sorbin's prostate.

When Sorbin didn't relax right away, Destrawn spread his wings and beat the air lightly, holding himself steady. That allowed him to wrap his arm around his mate's waist so he could find his cock. He gripped his mate's prick, concerned to find that it had slightly softened.

"I got you, my mate," Destrawn crooned into his ear as he began jacking him. "Sorry I rushed." Self-flagellation flooded him. "I'll fix it."

This is my mate, not some random fuck. What the hell am I doing?

Destrawn knew he should be showering Sorbin with kind words, sweet touches, and slow exploration. Instead, he was prepping him with speed, like some kind of uncontrolled adolescent—or a selfish asshole. Frowning, Destrawn began to pull his fingers free.

A low rumbling growl erupted from Sorbin. "What are you doing?" he demanded. "Don't you dare stop."

Freezing with just the tips of his fingers inside Sorbin's channel, Destrawn fought his warring instincts. He wanted to please his mate, but he wanted to care for him, too. His desire to begin bonding them clashed with his need to see to his care, too.

"I-I don't want to hurt you," Destrawn finally managed to say. "I shouldn't be rushing. I—" Getting his base instincts under control had never been so difficult in his life. "You're my mate. I'm supposed to take care of you."

Sorbin scoffed. "I'm also a grown-ass vampire, and I told you I could handle it." While clenching and relaxing his chute muscles around Destrawn's fingertips, he added, "Add more lube to your fingers and get them back in my ass, Dee. I need you."

Doing as he'd been told—which was a novel experience while in bed—Destrawn released Sorbin's cock. He picked up the lube, popped the cap, and poured a healthy dollop onto his fingers. After a second of hesitation, he squirted some onto his jerking, leaking erection, too.

Destrawn hissed as the cool slick slid down his dick, but the contrast helped ease his impending need for release. After dropping the tube on the comforter again, he pushed his fingers deep into Sorbin once more. His gut clenched anew when he felt the tight squeeze, so he grabbed the base of his own dick and squeezed . . . hard.

Even as Destrawn forced back his body's need to climax, he found Sorbin's prostate once more. He watched with satisfaction as a shudder rippled through the vampire. After teasing at the gland a couple more times just so he could hear his lover's groans of pleasure, Destrawn eased his fingers partway out, only to push them in again.

Releasing himself, Destrawn sprawled over Sorbin once more. He used his wings to balance his body, allowing him to grip his lover's erection once more. While jacking Sorbin's perfect handful of meat, he focused on stretching the vampire's chute.

Destrawn reveled in the way Sorbin moved beneath him. His vampire rocked back onto his fingers only to immediately thrust his hips. He knew the man was chasing his own pleasure, and Destrawn loved the wonderful flush darkening his flesh as well as the heady scent of arousal flooding the bedroom.

Using Sorbin's momentum, Destrawn finally worked a fourth finger into his vampire's body. His lover's movements stuttered an instant, then resumed. His chute rippled around Destrawn's digits, but they didn't tighten and no hint of pain entered Sorbin's scent.

"N-Now," Sorbin panted. "So damn close."

"Not until I'm in you," Destrawn stated before he could stay his natural dominance. "Want to feel you clench on my cock."

Sorbin nodded before resting his forehead on one clenched fist. "Do it," he urged. "I want that, too. Gonna milk you so good."

Destrawn groaned just at the thought. He couldn't help but do exactly that. Pulling his fingers free, he still remembered to be careful, to go slow so as not to hurt his lover — with his claws or by yanking out too fast along inner walls that had to have been sensitized by then.

Grabbing his dick, Destrawn jacked himself a few times, spreading the lube he'd dripped on himself and mixing it with what was left on his hand. He guided his swollen crown, his foreskin already peeled from the sensitive head, to Sorbin's prepared hole. With the pressure of his hips holding his head in place, Destrawn rested that hand on the comforter, unmindful of the lube clinging to his fingers.

"Push out, my mate," Destrawn urged as he nibbled at his nape. Adding a bit of pressure with his hips, he murmured, "I wish to feel your hot body envelope my cock. Give me what I want. Let me stroke your insides. Let me sheath myself within the confines of your body."

Destrawn had never considered himself a chatterer or talker during sex, but as he anticipated what was to come, he couldn't seem to shut up. His desire to feel his mate, to connect with him, drove every thought. His heart beat with the need to couple, to possess, to bury himself deep inside the vampire before him and stay there for as long as their stamina held out.

"You're mine, Sorbin," Destrawn continued. "You already know it. Give your body to me." Licking a stripe up Sorbin's neck, he mumbled, "Show me how you want my rod spearing your depths, plundering you. Milk me of my seed. Let me mark you inside and out."

Sorbin growled as he turned his head. His pale-blue irises

had bled to red, reminding Destrawn that he bedded a vampire . . . as if he could forget. Then Sorbin pinned him with a feral grin, his fangs on full display.

"If you don't thrust that spike you call a cock deep into my body in the next five seconds, I'm going to flip you over and ride you like a pogo stick."

Destrawn sucked in a harsh gasp upon hearing the rasp of Sorbin's voice. As much as he wanted to experience that, eventually, it wasn't what he needed right then. His dominance urged him to mount his mate, to demand his submission.

So Destrawn did as they both needed.

Pushing with his hips, Destrawn popped his crown past Sorbin's guardian muscle. He paused when he felt his lover clamp onto him. His breath left him in a hiss as he experienced the heat and squeeze of his soul mate for the first time.

Destrawn hadn't even gotten more than his crown in the vampire, and his balls were beginning to draw up. The base of his spine tingled, and his breathing became ragged. Groaning, Destrawn rested his forehead against Sorbin's nape, finding it sweaty and smelling delicious.

"Don't stop," Sorbin urged, rocking beneath him. "Bury your shaft in me. Split me open, beloved."

Upon hearing his vampire claim him, Destrawn felt his heart begin to thud wildly in his chest. His skin beaded with sweat. Losing control in the face of Sorbin's urgings, Destrawn thrust . . . hard.

In one long, smooth glide, Destrawn buried his erection balls deep in his mate. The hot pressure wrapped around his prick, encasing him in the sweetest cocoon he'd ever experienced. To his shock, a shudder racked him, how exquisite he found being embedded in his mate.

"S-Sorbin," Destrawn groaned.

Unable to control his hips, he pulled out, only to slam back into his lover. The sweet massage of his vampire's inner walls working the skin of his dick nearly caused his eyes to roll to the back of his head. Wrapping his arms around his mate, he used his wings to lever them both onto his knees, until he sat back on his calves with Sorbin sprawled on his lap.

"Hands behind my neck," Destrawn ordered when he felt Sorbin shift on his lap. "Now."

Satisfaction flooded Destrawn when Sorbin obeyed. His vampire lifted his arms, hanging onto him. Licking and sucking the side of Sorbin's neck, he admired the lean, toned male sprawled on him.

Sorbin's body was flushed pink with his arousal, and gleamed with sweat, making him almost appear to glow. His chest heaved, and his nipples were beaded. He rested his head against Destrawn's shoulder, and his eyes were heavy-lidded, glazed with lust.

Destrawn slid one arm around his upper torso, palming it in a way so he could tease his thumb and fingers over both nipples. His vampire groaned for his trouble. He continued to work the nubs, reveling in the sounds erupting from his lover's mouth.

Trailing the claws of his other hand down Sorbin's abdominals, Destrawn enjoyed the way they fluttered under his touch. When he reached his vampire's straining prick, he teased around the base. As his lover's cock jerked and twitched, waving as if for attention, Destrawn relished the breathy whines escaping Sorbin's lips. When he carefully cradled his vampire's balls and gave them a light, experimental squeeze, his vampire barked his name and arched, as if searching for friction on his leaking dick.

All the while, Destrawn kept his own erection buried deep inside Sorbin's body. He knew if he moved an inch, he would erupt, and he needed his mate to come first. His balls were so heavy with seed, he could barely control himself.

With that thought in mind, Destrawn released his lover's testicles. He scraped his claws down then up the soft skin of Sorbin's inner thigh. Then he wrapped his fingers around his vampire's erection and began jacking, firm and sure.

"Dee!" Sorbin cried, his body seizing in his arms. Shudders jolted his vampire, and Destrawn felt his lover's claws pricking the back of his neck. "D-Dee. D-Dee. S-So close."

Growling not only at the nickname—no one had ever given him one before, not that he would have allowed it—but at the sound of Sorbin's whimpers, cries, and moans, coupled with the way he trembled in his arms.

"Do it," Destrawn demanded. "Come for your mate. Spill your seed all over my hand." As he watched another bead of pre-cum ooze from Sorbin's flared red crown, Destrawn's mouth watered. "I want to taste you. Spray your cum into my hand, so I may enjoy your sweet flavor."

Then Destrawn nipped at his shoulder. Not hard enough to draw blood, that would come soon, but it was hard enough to stimulate his mate. It did just that, too.

Sorbin roared. His body arched. The erection in Destrawn's hand jerked and pulsed, pumping cum from his body. The first burst arced through the air like a beautiful fountain and splattered on Sorbin's destroyed polo. Destrawn adjusted his hand to catch the next spurt.

Destrawn ground his teeth as Sorbin's inner muscles clenched and released on his embedded prick. His gut tightened, and he could no longer fight his need. As his orgasm swamped him, his instincts raged.

Opening his mouth, Destrawn wrapped his jaw around the point where Sorbin's neck met his shoulder. He bit, sinking his sharp teeth deep into his flesh. Blood oozed up around his teeth, filling his mouth and flowing across his tongue.

Moaning at the delicious nectar igniting his taste buds in the best possible way, Destrawn reveled in the exquisite taste.

He sucked on the flesh, needing more of his vampire's delectable life fluid. His senses swam as his bliss of release combined with knowing they'd begun their bond.

When Sorbin wrapped his hand around Destrawn's wrist, he barely registered the contact. He didn't fight his mate when the vampire lifted his arm. The prick of Sorbin's teeth roused him a little, but the slide of his vampire's sharp fangs into his flesh caused him to tense.

Then the headiest sensations shot through his blood, spreading fiery tendrils through his body. His nipples beaded, his blood thudded through his veins, and he tipped his head back and roared. Ecstasy caused black spots to flash across his vision, and he barely hung onto consciousness as Sorbin sucked on his wrist for several long heartbeats that seemed to go on and on.

When Sorbin finally eased his fangs free and licked the mark clean, Destrawn's chest heaved as if he'd run a marathon. His body felt wrung out in a way he'd never before experienced. Even his balls ached as if they'd been turned inside out.

Sighing, Destrawn blinked open eyes he couldn't remember closing and peered down at Sorbin. He winced upon seeing the open wound on his vampire's shoulder. When his mate had bitten him, any thought but the pleasure had gone out of his head.

Destrawn dipped his head and gently lapped around the torn flesh. Carefully, he cleaned around it, all the while murmuring his apologies. "So sorry, my mate. Didn't mean to leave you like this." When Destrawn had it sealed, he stared at it.

Unable to help himself, Destrawn had to smile at the massive claiming scar he'd left in his mate's flesh.

Just damn. Everyone is going to see that any time he's not wearing a shirt with a high collar.

"Feeling smug?"

Shifting his gaze to Sorbin's face, Destrawn saw the smirk on the vampire's lips. Pleased his mate didn't appear, or scent, of upset, he admitted the truth.

"More like satisfied," Destrawn revealed. "More satisfied than I've ever been in my life."

CHAPTER SIX

While Sorbin's shoulder had throbbed, he never would have complained. He knew the effects caused by a vampire bite, and from what he'd heard, the bite to a beloved was even more intense. Besides, when his gargoyle had yanked his teeth free and roared his name, Sorbin had felt more satisfaction than he'd ever felt in his life.

I did that. I made my dominant beloved lose control with bliss.

Feeling Destrawn tighten one arm around his torso, then begin to pitch forward, Sorbin expected him to pull out. The gargoyle didn't. Instead, he carefully lowered them both to their sides, maneuvering them both out of the wet spot.

Destrawn kept his slightly softened cock still in Sorbin's chute as he curled up around his back. The gargoyle spread one huge black wing over them, then hummed. After kissing Sorbin's nape, he lifted onto his elbow.

To Sorbin's surprise, he realized that Destrawn somehow still held a palm full of cum. His beloved brought it to his lips and sipped. As he watched, the gargoyle drank every last bit of his seed, then licked his palm clean.

With a sigh, Destrawn settled back behind him. When he met Sorbin's gaze, a lascivious smile curved his lips. He winked, then wiped his damp hand on the soiled and ruined polo shirt.

Just as quickly, Destrawn's eyebrow ridges furrowed and a serious expression crossed his face. He tucked his head against Sorbin's nape. Letting out a long sigh, he rubbed his palm over Sorbin's stomach.

46

Sorbin rested his hand on Destrawn's wrist, surprised to find quite a bit of tension on the gargoyle's arm. Squeezing lightly, he asked, "Is everything okay?" He clenched his chute muscles lightly, massaging his beloved's still-embedded length. Putting a note of teasing in his tone, Sorbin asked, "Still need something?"

Destrawn growled as he tightened his arm. "Just need to feel connected to you when I share this," came the surprising response.

Frowning, Sorbin turned his head a little, trying to catch Destrawn's eye. His beloved had his face hidden in his hair, hiding his features. That didn't stop him from catching a rising smell of unease from Destrawn.

"Heyyyy," Sorbin crooned, rubbing up and down Destrawn's forearm. "I'm not upset about the bite. Really." He wasn't certain what else could be the problem. "Besides." Sorbin chuckled. "It made me shoot like a rocket. You can bite me anytime."

Destrawn sighed again before pecking a kiss to Sorbin's nape. "That's not what I'm thinking about."

Sorbin cast about for something else. "Uh, I'm sure you know vampires and their beloveds normally end up forming a mind-link, but it's not like I can read it." Threading his fingers between Destrawn's, he squeezed lightly. "And I don't know if it will form until after we've finished the bond."

"Good to know, my mate," Destrawn rumbled, nuzzling his nose along his neck and snuffling deeply, perhaps searching for comfort. "You asked if I've ever bottomed. The short answer is yes, but it wasn't by choice."

With those unexpected words, Sorbin felt as if he'd been sucker-punched.

Surely I'm jumping to conclusions. Surely, Destrawn doesn't mean that the way it sounded.

As if Destrawn could indeed read Sorbin's mind, even though he'd just said that wasn't how a vampire link worked, the gargoyle rumbled, "Yes, that is how it sounds." Heaving a deep sigh, he muttered, "But it probably didn't happen quite like you'd imagine."

"Uhhhh," Sorbin began, but he didn't know where to go with that. Instead, he finished, "Please know you don't have to tell me anything you don't want to."

Destrawn grunted as he shifted behind him, as if he could cuddle up any closer. "No, I want to," he claimed. "It'll help you . . . understand."

Sorbin nodded, then rested the back of his head against Destrawn's shoulder, offering another point of connection. "I'll listen to anything you have to say," he promised.

After another grunt, Destrawn took a deep breath. He let it out, then took another one.

It was then that Sorbin realized his gargoyle was taking comfort, and maybe even strength, from his scent and their connection. He relaxed and waited. As he listened to the bigger male breathe, he vowed to wait as long as it took until his beloved was ready to talk . . . even if that was never.

At least now, his hesitance to bottom makes sense if the first time he was . . . forced.

"You have to remember," Destrawn began, his words slow. "It was a different time back then."

"Back when?" Sorbin's natural curiosity had him blurting out the question before he could think better of it. "Sorry," he amended. "Um, ignore me."

Destrawn chuckled, much to Sorbin's surprise. The gargoyle nibbled at his earlobe as he rubbed his hips against his ass cheeks. Then he licked over his claiming bite on Sorbin's neck.

"A little hard to ignore you, my mate," Destrawn growled. "And you may ask me anything." He nudged his forehead against Sorbin, a move that he was quickly coming to realize was a mixture of affection and hiding. "Sometimes, it may just take me longer to answer than others. I've been alone a long,

long time."

"Okay." Sorbin could work with that.

Destrawn hummed for a few seconds, his arm tightening a bit before relaxing. "I was hatched in the summer of fourteen-eighty-seven to a clutch that was run by a gargoyle who was on par with most in those times, but he was old and out of touch with most of what went on in the clutch." As if needing the contact, Destrawn began petting over Sorbin's stomach, tracing his abdominal grooves. "He left most of the day to day shit with his second, who . . . used manipulation and sex to keep people in line."

"Shit," Sorbin muttered. He bet that hadn't gone over well with Destrawn's dominant personality.

While his chuckle sounded a little strained, Destrawn nodded. "Yeah. Guess he realized I would end up damn dominant, and he wanted to make certain I was . . . under his thumb, so to speak . . . from day one."

For a long moment, Destrawn remained quiet, and Sorbin had to bite his tongue to ask what happened.

Finally, Destrawn started speaking again. "Gargoyles are inherently bisexual. As a race, we've always known that. And remember, in the fourteen hundreds, age of consent was a lot younger than it is now . . . or not at all if the marriage was arranged by the parents."

Sorbin hesitated, then offered, "Okay."

"Guess I questioned my father one too many times," Destrawn told him. "Because, one day, when I was fourteen, I came home from doing chores, and Second Morland was waiting in our rooms. He was alone."

When the bitter scent of anger and frustration teased at Sorbin's senses, he knew what was coming. He wished he could tell Destrawn to stop, that he didn't have to say it. Except, he'd told his beloved that he would listen if he wished to share. With that thought in mind, Sorbin rubbed up and down Destrawn's arm, doing his best to soothe his gargoyle as he relived those memories.

"In those days, it wasn't unheard of for an older male to introduce a younger to the ways of sex." Destrawn's voice came out even, flat almost, as if he were relaying a history lesson instead of his own past. "And that's what Morland did, showing me how to be good at receiving. How to submit and take care of the more dominant."

Destrawn fell silent, and after a moment passed, Sorbin realized he'd lost himself in the memories.

Sorbin racked his brain for a way to help Destrawn. Since his lover's chosen position wasn't doing it, he knew they needed a change. Taking a chance, Sorbin eased his hips forward, drawing his ass away from Destrawn's groin. It didn't take much for his lover's softened prick to slip free of his body, telling Sorbin exactly how much the gargoyle was affected by what he shared.

Ignoring the rush of seed that dribbled from him, Sorbin eased onto his back. He spotted Destrawn's vacant expression immediately, and the haunted look nearly broke his heart. Needing to erase that as swiftly as possible, he reached for his beloved.

Sorbin slid his left arm underneath Destrawn's big torso. At the same, he gripped his shoulder. Then he pulled his gargoyle toward him, encouraging him to sprawl over his body, all the while thanking the fact that he had vampire strength.

Sliding his hand up from Destrawn's shoulder to his jaw, Sorbin urged his beloved to lift his gaze. He pressed a light kiss to the gargoyle's thick lips. After another couple of brushes, along with a swipe of Sorbin's tongue and a nibble to Destrawn's lower lip, he felt his gargoyle begin to reciprocate.

Teasing and lapping, they shared a slow, exploratory kiss. There was no hurry in their actions, just a languid exchange of mutual enjoyment.

Finally, Destrawn slid his fingers into Sorbin's hair and drew the kiss to an end. He lifted his head and stared down at him, his gaze warm with a different kind of heat — affection. His lips were curved in a smile, and his gray eyes had lightened, betraying the fact that it wasn't arousal he was feeling, but something else, perhaps something more.

"Thank you, Sorbin," Destrawn rumbled gruffly. "For pulling me out of . . . that."

Sorbin rubbed gently along the column of Destrawn's neck, enjoying the slightly mottled hide beneath his fingertips. He knew he would never get tired of their differences. The look of contentment the move created on Destrawn's face would probably have something to do with that, too.

"You're my beloved, Destrawn," Sorbin stated quietly. "I'll always try to support you." Grimacing, he added, "And I don't want to see you in pain, physical or mental." Sorbin decided to offer, "I get the gist, so if you don't want to continue, I understand."

Destrawn grunted even as he shook his head. Sliding closer, he flung one leg over Sorbin's thighs while teasing his claws across his scalp. Keeping his weight on his right arm, the gargoyle told him, "Let's just say, when he was done, he'd thought he trained me in submission and being a good little clutch-member, but it didn't actually have the effect he'd intended." His expression hardened a bit, and he stared off to the left. "I was quieter, more subservient, sure, but that was on the outside. On the inside, I watched how people interacted with each other. I became a master at spotting the difference between those that were genuine and those that were manipulators." Destrawn met Sorbin's gaze again, and a smirk curved his lips. "I made a detailed log, and even discovered how Second Morland took the virginity of every single clutch-member — male or female — when they turned fourteen. He probably manipulated my parents into making them think it was necessary, because I heard him doing the same to a set of parents with a daughter. I reported his activities to the Circle of Elders."

"Damn!" Sorbin rubbed up and down Destrawn's strong back, impressed with not only his physical strength but his mental fortitude. "What happened to him?"

Destrawn grinned, the look one of dark smugness. "I heard he went through a reeducation program, then was assigned to a new clutch." His eyes narrowed. "When he continued to try the same shit, his new chieftain punished him, repeatedly. He never held a position of power again, became bitter, tried to stage a coup on his clutch, and ended up killed for his trouble."

Sorbin gaped. "Damn."

Clearing his expression, Destrawn nodded. "That's not the important part, though."

While Sorbin wasn't so certain, he nodded anyway. "Okay."

"What I'm trying to say is." Destrawn paused and sighed deeply. After nuzzling at Sorbin's temple, he whispered, "I always knew if I met my mate in a man, there was a possibility that he would enjoy topping, too. And that the quickest and least painful way to go through molt was to bottom for him, then keep him close so his flesh could soothe mine."

Sorbin hadn't known that, but he kept quiet.

"Anyway, I will bottom for you, Sorbin," Destrawn told him. His brow ridges furrowed a bit as his look turned troubled. "I'm just . . . going to need . . . a little time. Maybe" — the scent of his embarrassment filled the air — "a bit of play first? T-To, um, experience how good it can be?"

For a second, Sorbin had trouble processing Destrawn's request. Time was understandable enough.

Butt play?

Then it hit Sorbin.

"You haven't even played with yourself since then?"

Destrawn shook his head. "What he did" — his features tightened, but he plowed ahead — "it was all about the bottom pleasing the top. I didn't learn how to care for my partner for . . . a long damn time." His eyes held a wealth of sadness as he admitted, "For my first couple of centuries, I was a shit lover."

Sorbin got it. Really, he did.

Squeezing Destrawn's neck, Sorbin whispered, "You didn't know any better."

"I *should* have," Destrawn grumbled, pressing his face against Sorbin's neck once more. "I should *never* have treated a lover the way that asshole treated me." As he spoke, he levered over Sorbin, pushing between his thighs. "Gods, you smell fucking fantastic. How can I be talking about this and be getting hard?"

Groaning, Sorbin welcomed Destrawn between his thighs. He felt his gargoyle's thick rod pressing against him, and his own dick immediately responded. Planting his feet, Sorbin rocked, showing his beloved that he was in the same state.

As they frotted slowly, Sorbin recalled Destrawn's question and gave the short answer. "Because we haven't completed our bond, yet." He turned his head and nipped at his gargoyle's pointed ear, then suckled on the tip of the appendage.

Destrawn hissed and grabbed Sorbin's thigh, using the hold to lift his leg, giving the gargoyle more access. "Godsssss, that's fucking good," he rumbled, doing some nibbling of his own. A definite whine entered his voice as he urged, "Don't stop."

Sorbin realized he'd just found another hot spot. Happy to heighten his gargoyle's pleasure, he obeyed. While continuing to tease his tongue around the pointed tip and down the side of Destrawn's ear, Sorbin slid his hands down the gargoyle's back and found his wings.

Feeling the shudder that worked through Destrawn caused a surge of pride to flood Sorbin. He also bet that the shivering man in his arms had never before made the rumbling cries of pleasure currently escaping him. Their sweat-slicked bodies sliding together caused the best kind of friction, and Sorbin did a little moaning of his own.

Feeling his lover's erection slide down his balls, then slip beneath him, Sorbin knew what was coming. He rocked his hips, helping to get Destrawn's cock head right where they both needed. As his gargoyle sank into him once more, Sorbin sighed and pushed out, welcoming his lover into his body.

Destrawn lifted his head once he was fully seated inside him. His eyes had once again darkened to the shade of storm clouds, and hunger was etched across his features. With his lips peeled away from his sharp teeth, his fierce expression should have caused Sorbin concern, but all it did was send a fresh wash of excitement through him.

I did that. I made this strong male lose himself with need.

"I'll bottom for you, Sorbin," Destrawn told him as he began drawing his dick out of his chute. "I promise I will."

Sorbin tightened his arms around Destrawn's shoulders and rocked into each delicious stroke. "We have all the time in the world."

Groaning, Destrawn lowered his head and captured Sorbin's mouth, ravishing him in the best possible ways.

CHAPTER SEVEN

The chime of a phone pulled Destrawn out of the light doze he'd been in. After the second round with Sorbin, they'd both stumbled into the shower. Their clean-up had been quick and perfunctory before they'd returned to Sorbin's bed, stripped the sheets, and climbed under the comforter to pass out in post-coital bliss.

As Destrawn attempted to pinpoint the sound, he realized he couldn't remember the last time he'd slept with a lover.

Hell, it's been centuries.

Destrawn spotted a phone half in and half out of Sorbin's pocket. By then, the ringing had stopped, so he began to settle his head back onto the pillow. Except, then the phone began to ring again.

Glancing at Sorbin, seeing that he still slept, Destrawn eased one wing from around him. He bent his appendage awkwardly, reaching it downward. Using a hook on one of his topline joints, Destrawn grabbed the fabric and hauled it to him.

After removing the phone from the jeans' pocket, Destrawn dropped them back to the floor. He read the name of the caller — Lathe. Recalling that Sorbin had called him a brother by bond, he decided to accept the call.

"Sorbin's phone," Destrawn rumbled softly, keeping his voice down in the hopes of giving his mate more time to sleep. Considering the vampire had been out on assignment, he guessed he hadn't gotten much sleep of late. When Destrawn didn't hear anything other than breathing, he asked, "Lathe?

Is something wrong?" Realizing the vampire had no reason to tell him since he didn't know him, he tried, "This is Destrawn, Sorbin's beloved. He's catching up on sleep, at the moment. Can I help you?"

"Sorbin doesn't have a beloved," a soft tenor stated coldly. "Who are you really? What have you done with him?" The man's voice hardened even further as he barked into the phone, "Are you a priest? If you harm one hair on Sorbin's head, I will—"

"Whoa, whoa! Lathe, calm down," Sorbin called, having woken at some point during Lathe's rant. He grabbed the phone from Destrawn, an apologetic look on his face. "I'm here," he stated, placing the phone at his ear. Sorbin rested his other ear back on Destrawn's chest, saying, "I'm fine. Destrawn isn't a priest. I promise."

"Are you sure?" Lathe asked warily. "You're not just saying that?" Before Sorbin could reply, Lathe quickly added, "Because I looked out the window, and it looked like rain."

Arching one brow in silent question, Destrawn wondered what the hell Lathe was talking about.

Sorbin's smile turned pained, but he didn't do anything to try to hide their conversation, which he had to know Destrawn could hear every word of.

"No, it's not going to rain today, Lathe," Sorbin replied in a soft tone. "The sky is blue here, and let me tell you, there are some real big puffy clouds out there."

For at least half a minute, Lathe remained quiet on the other end.

When Destrawn opened his mouth to ask what was going on, Sorbin lifted his free hand and touched it to his lips, staying his words. Unable to help himself, Destrawn flicked out his tongue, happy to taste the light salt on his mate's fingertips. Sorbin smiled wryly at him, so Destrawn winked back.

"You're serious," Lathe finally whispered.

"I am," Sorbin confirmed.

After another few heartbeats, Lathe asked softly, "Is Destrawn really your beloved?"

Sorbin smiled at Destrawn as he lowered his hand and rubbed over his chest. "Yes, Destrawn is my beloved. He's a gargoyle here from the Aerasceatle clutch." Grinning with pleasure filling his tone, Sorbin continued, "I would have told you and the guys earlier, but I met him at the conference when I gave Master Krispin my report. Then we went to my suite to talk, and one thing led to another and" — Sorbin paused to clear his throat before finishing — "everything caught up with me, and I sorta passed out."

"The Aerasceatle clutch," Lathe repeated slowly. "Those are the gargoyles nearby, right? Your beloved is a gargoyle?"

"Right," Sorbin confirmed. "Destrawn is the second in the clutch there."

Destrawn couldn't help but smile, pleased at how proud Sorbin sounded.

Lathe's deep sigh came through the line. "So, you're leaving me. I guess I always knew you would eventually."

"Actually, I was going to offer in person," Sorbin quickly countered. "But I confirmed that you could join me . . . if you wanted to."

"Really?" Lathe sounded shocked. "Why? I mean, why would they allow that? We're not actually blood."

Sorbin snorted. "Maybe not, but we're brothers by bond. We've been through a lot together." Holding Destrawn's gaze, his voice ringing with sincerity, Sorbin stated, "Lathe, finding my beloved is not going to change our relationship."

After a few more seconds, Lathe stated, "I'll think about it."

Sorbin winced, but he seemed to accept that. "What time is it?"

"Almost two-thirty AM," Lathe replied.

"Ah, Vic must have gotten off security about a half-hour

ago, huh?"

Destrawn made a note to ask who that was later.

"Yeah. We were gonna have a few drinks and some food while scoping out the bar. He said you might meet us there."

"Uhhhh." Sorbin peered at Destrawn uncertainly. While he could see the desire to see his friends in Sorbin's eyes, his vampire answered, "I can't. Uh, Destrawn and I just met, so of course, he doesn't have a human form. I—"

As much as Destrawn wanted to keep his mate by his side, seeing as he'd just met him, he wanted the vampire happy, too. Plus, he would be perfectly safe within the confines of the coven.

"If you wish to meet up with your friends, I won't stop you, my mate," Destrawn told him, cutting into the conversation. He figured Lathe would be able to hear him just fine through the line, being a vampire. "I can call my chieftain and make arrangements for moving. I'll check available single suites, too, just in case Lathe decides to join you."

"Wait a minute." A new, deeper voice came through the line. "Did someone just say mate? What the hell is going on?"

"Sorbin met his beloved," Lathe supplied. Either the vampire had put the phone on speaker, or the newcomer was also a paranormal.

"Hot damn!" a third voice cried. While also a tenor, there was a definite note of confidence that Lathe's tone did not possess. "You found your beloved, Sorbin? That's fantastic! Congratulations." The man's jovial tone flooded the line. "Bring him on down. We wanna meet him."

"Thanks, Donny," Sorbin replied, identifying the speaker. "And Destrawn is a gargoyle, so we can't make it to the bar. He says I can—"

"A gargoyle? Say no more," the first interloper interrupted. "We're on our way with the good stuff. We'll order up."

Just that fast, the line disconnected.

Sorbin looked about as shell-shocked as Destrawn felt.

"Uh, guess you're about to meet my best friends, Vicon and Donny," Sorbin told him. "As well as my brother from another mother, Lathe." Pulling away, he swung his legs over the side of his bed. He paused and half-turned back to face him. "Uh, about Lathe . . . try not to stare or question. Okay? I'll explain later, but I can guarantee we don't have much time until they arrive."

Destrawn really wanted to ask questions, but from the way Sorbin was swiftly yanking on his jeans and finding a new shirt, he figured they really didn't have that much time.

After tying his loincloth back into place, Destrawn pulled the comforter back and shook it out. He spotted his hairband as it dropped to the floor. After spreading the blanket back over the mattress — ignoring the need for sheets — Destrawn grabbed the band and finger-combed his hair before tying it back from his face.

Then Destrawn exited the bedroom and smiled upon seeing Sorbin hurrying around the front room, straightening it up. When they'd first arrived there, he'd wondered if his mate was inherently messy. Then the vampire had blushed and explained that he hadn't been there for more than a change of clothes and a quick bite to eat in almost four days.

Destrawn helped clear the dishes off the coffee table and piled them onto a rolling tray that had most likely come from the coven kitchens. Then he took it and wheeled it toward the door. Just as Destrawn was placing it in the hallway for pickup, he heard the ding of the elevator.

Turning back toward the room, Destrawn heard a wolf whistle. He paused and turned, arching one brow ridge. Spotting the trio of vampires heading toward him, he figured these were his mate's friends.

The tallest stood six-foot-four with a wiry, rangy frame. He had dark hair and eyes. His gaze swept over Destrawn in a clearly assessing manner as he eyed him with interest, and he carried a large paper sack in his arms.

Judging from the smell filling the hallway, it contained food—including some kind of baked item that clearly held cinnamon. Destrawn fought back a smirk, not at all surprised that the vampires in the coven knew how to prevent gargoyle pregnancy. After all, through a lack of communication, Master Krispin had already ended up pregnant by Wash and had given birth to an egg.

The second male, a light-brown-haired vampire, stood an inch or so shorter and carried a bottle of some sort of alcohol. His shoulders were quite a bit broader, and he had what Destrawn had been told were classically handsome, boy-next-door features that probably made it easy to woo, well, whoever he wanted. He also had hazel eyes that were lit up with happiness, and he smiled broadly at Destrawn.

The final vampire wouldn't reach six feet in his stocking feet and had a slender frame. He hung back a little, limping on his left side. His black hair was shorn nearly scalp-close on his right side while hanging to his chin on the left. Still, Destrawn's keen eyesight allowed him to make out the scarring on his left cheek beneath the strands.

Interesting. Something traumatic must have happened to cause an injury that severe on a vampire.

That must be Lathe.

Recalling Sorbin's warning, Destrawn resisted the urge to stare . . . or ask. He focused on the grinning male. "I'm guessing you're Sorbin's friends?" He held out his hand to the tawny-haired vampire. "I'm Destrawn."

"Destrawn, huh?" the vampire replied, taking his hand. "Donny." After releasing, he used a thumb to point at the dark-brown-haired man, then the black-haired one. "Vicon and Lathe." He held up a bottle of tequila. "Let's go get to know each other."

Nodding, Destrawn led the way back into Sorbin's suite.

Destrawn couldn't remember the last time he'd ended up answering so many prying questions.

Peering around at all the sleeping vampires in the front room, Destrawn shook his head. He knew they hadn't drank enough tequila to actually pass out from it, but that, combined with the late hour, had Sorbin's three friends zonked out on the sofas and chairs.

"Sorry about all that," Sorbin murmured, coming up behind him and wrapping his arms around his waist. "Thank you for handling their curiosity so well."

Shrugging, Destrawn turned as he replied, "They're your friends." He wrapped his arms around Sorbin and peered into his mate's pale-blue eyes.

Sorbin smiled up at him, the lines around his mouth betraying his fatigue. "When I get to your clutch, am I going to go through an inquisition from some of your friends?"

Destrawn shook his head. "No. I don't really have friends there, per se." Seeing Sorbin's frown and scenting his confusion, he admitted, "As second of a recuperating clutch, I haven't gotten close to anyone but the inner circle. They won't question you about your suitability to stay with me." Smirking, Destrawn told him, "Hell, they'll probably be giving you advice on how to tolerate my demanding nature."

Rolling his eyes, Sorbin claimed, "I'm sure I can handle it."

Chuckling, Destrawn nodded. "I'm certain you can."

Then Destrawn lowered his head and sealed his lips over Sorbin's own. He teased them apart with his tongue before delving inside. Tasting tequila, spicy hot wings, potato skins, cinnamon twists, and underneath that, his vampire's unique masculine flavor, Destrawn relished the opportunity to just explore and savor.

In the past, Destrawn had always used kissing as a means to an end. He'd used it to arouse a lover or seduce someone.

Now he did it simply because he enjoyed sharing the activity with his mate.

Destrawn felt Sorbin sway a little and eased the kiss to an end. Seeing the glazed look on his vampire's face, he grinned. He knew part of that was from fatigue. His hard-working tracker was far from recovered.

Deciding he knew the perfect way to put Sorbin to bed, Destrawn wrapped his arm around his vampire's waist. He guided him into the bedroom, closing the door behind them. Pausing beside the bed, he pulled Sorbin's clothes from his body.

After pulling the comforter back down, Destrawn helped Sorbin onto the mattress. He made a mental note to discover where his mate kept his sheets another time. Right then, he had something else on his mind.

Climbing onto the bed beside Sorbin, Destrawn buried his face in his vampire's crotch. He inhaled deeply, nuzzling his nose against the man's half-hard prick. His delicious aroma immediately caused Destrawn's blood to fire, and his cock thickened behind his loincloth.

This wasn't about his own pleasure however, so he ignored it.

After licking gently all over Sorbin's balls, enjoying the sound of his lover's groans and grunts, reveling in how he spread his legs wantonly for him, Destrawn went for what he really wanted.

Destrawn opened his mouth and swallowed Sorbin's erection to the root. His mate's masculine goodness saturated his tongue as his ears registered his vampire's deep groan.

Grinning around his perfect mouthful of meat, Destrawn set to work driving his vampire out of his mind.

CHAPTER EIGHT

Sorbin roused slowly, instinctively reaching across the sheets for his beloved. As he had the last three mornings, he came up empty. The sheets were cool.

Blinking open his eyelids, he saw the light shining around the edges of the curtains, which told him the day was in full swing. He eased to a sitting position and peered around the room. His gaze focused on the statue in the corner—his beloved on one knee, his wings wrapped around him, and his head bowed.

Sighing, Sorbin rubbed his hands over his face. He knew it was possible for a gargoyle to suck off his male mate enough to go through molt. Sorbin didn't know if that was what Destrawn was aiming for or not, since he put him to sleep with a blowjob every night, and they hadn't discussed Sorbin topping again.

Sorbin understood that he was the less dominant one, and he knew why Destrawn hesitated to give him his ass. It conjured bad memories for him. He just wished he could help his beloved replace them with good ones of their own.

Plus, Sorbin's vampire nature was beginning to ride him hard to claim Destrawn properly.

Pushing from the bed, Sorbin did his best to put those thoughts aside. He headed to the bathroom and went about his morning routine. As he'd done the prior morning, he marveled at the nicely appointed ensuite.

Sorbin and Destrawn had stayed at the coven for the first

forty-eight hours. Ignoring the threat of attack from paranormal haters for a half a day, his people had put together a going away slash congratulations party. While he'd noticed Destrawn had been a bit out of his element, his beloved had stuck it out.

Lathe had been a little uncomfortable, too, sticking to the edge of the festivities. Sorbin had done his best to visit with him often, and one of their buddies had always stayed with him. Even Destrawn had hung out with Lathe for a while.

To Sorbin's surprise—and pleasure—Lathe had agreed to move to the clutch with them. He hadn't arrived, yet, but they expected him just after the New Year's party. Destrawn had made the suggestion since they were uncertain of their clutch's safety while rounding up hunters. He'd used the excuse of setting up a kick-ass electronics office for him, since Master Krispin had assigned Lathe with looking into Lady Alexa Milligan and anything hunter related.

After moving to the clutch, Sorbin had wanted to head into Lake Point and poke around, but Destrawn had kyboshed the idea. He refused to have his mate wandering around the town by himself. When Lionad had offered to escort him, Destrawn had nearly taken the tracker's head off.

Sorbin hadn't brought it up again.

As he couldn't do his job, he used the time to recover from his last one. He also worked remotely with Lathe, who was an excellent hacker, to see what they could dig up on the humans his coven had managed to identify. So far, they had names and pictures for five hunters, but according to hotel records—at least the ones done online—none of them had a room in town.

That meant aliases, which they didn't know.

After dressing, Sorbin headed out of the suite. He'd given himself a tour of the place the first day, and he felt pretty confident getting around. His stomach growled, and he smiled in anticipation.

The gargoyle dining hall always seemed to have a great spread available.

Sorbin reached the room and searched out a familiar face. He spotted Lionad's human mate, Simon. After waving at the small male, he headed to the buffet to get some food.

With a tray in hand, including a cinnamon roll, Sorbin headed to Simon's table to enjoy his breakfast.

Hearing the alarm sound on his phone, Sorbin turned his focus from his computer. He blinked a couple of times, then reached for his phone. Seeing that it was almost sunset, he turned off the alarm and placed it back on the desk.

Sorbin rose from his seat, then stretched his arms over his head. Just as his back popped pleasantly, he heard a ding come from his computer. He rested one hand on the desk and grabbed the mouse with the other.

After a click of the button, upon seeing the information displayed, Sorbin grinned widely and sat back down. He pulled up the database used by a Lake Point bed and breakfast and scanned the information. It seemed a Mister and Misses Reginald Milligan had registered there. They would be checking in the following afternoon.

Well, well, well. Seems you're a bit self-confident, aren't you?

Sorbin quickly passed the information on to Chieftain Kinsey while copying Master Krispin. His first inclination was to head out there immediately and scout the area. He itched to get the lay of the land.

Knowing that wasn't an available option to him, he did the next best thing. He pulled up a street map of the town and the outlying area. Scanning the area, he discovered the location of the bed and breakfast as well as other hotels, plus he figured out where each hiking trail was.

When Sorbin began pulling up topographical maps for hiking trails, his phone beeped, telling him he had a text message.

Upon seeing it was from Destrawn, Sorbin grimaced. "Shit." He realized he'd gotten distracted too long. Dialing his beloved, Sorbin locked his computer, then rose from his seat.

"You're not in our suite," Destrawn growled possessively. "Where are you?"

"In the tech office," Sorbin admitted. He knew Lathe would love the place. He'd told his tech-savvy friend about the space, and how the chieftain had offered to get whatever he and Lathe needed to bring them into the twenty-first century. "I'll be there soon."

Destrawn sighed. "Sorry to growl. Just miss you when you're not here when I wake from roost."

Sorbin spoke without thinking. "Well, if you went through molt, you wouldn't be stuck in roost all day." Grimacing, he slapped his hand over his mouth.

"What?"

While Sorbin figured Destrawn's one word question was a knee-jerk reaction, he grimaced. "I-I'm sorry. I shouldn't have—" Sorbin paused, but when his beloved didn't say anything, he heaved a sigh. "I'll be there in a minute."

"No," Destrawn rumbled deeply. "Meet me in the dining hall. I'd like a cup of coffee before we have this conversation."

When Destrawn hung up, not allowing Sorbin an answer, he hung his head. "Fuck," he muttered. Knowing he'd screwed that up, he shoved his phone in his pocket and did as his beloved had asked. He went to the dining hall.

Upon reaching the space, Sorbin couldn't bring himself to bother getting a plate of food. His stomach was too tied up in knots to digest anything. Instead, he poured himself a glass of white wine and headed toward an empty table off to the side.

Before Sorbin reached it, someone grabbed his upper arm. He turned and stared down at one of the smaller gargoyles of the clutch. Sorbin had noticed the tan-hided gargoyle with white claws staring at him a time or two—normally with a scowl on his face—but this was the first time the male had approached.

"Destrawn isn't your beloved," the guy declared with a sneer. "Why do you keep up with this façade? Why don't you just go back to your coven?"

Taken aback by the vehemence in the gargoyle's hissed comment, it took Sorbin a second to answer. "Be careful gargoyle," he warned softly. Knowing the smaller of their kind had been abused for decades, he didn't want to get the guy into trouble if he was just confused. "It's sacrosanct to come between a fated pair. Don't bring yourself trouble."

"Maybe I'd be concerned if you were actually a fated pair, but we both know differently, don't we?" The guy's smirk appeared condescending. "What's your game? Couldn't get a leg up in your coven, so you decided to go for a gargoyle?" Scoffing, he added, "No wonder Destrawn won't let you claim him. What do you have on him? Hmm?"

Yanking his hand free, Sorbin felt anger begin to simmer in his veins. "Be careful of what you speak," he snapped, fighting back a blush. "My bonding with my beloved is none of your damn business."

Shit. Do other gargoyles share this one's thoughts?

"I'll figure it out," the gargoyle declared, scowling at him with anger glinting in his hazel eyes. "You'll be sorry if you don't get out of here."

Then the gargoyle spun and stalked toward an exit to the left.

For several seconds, even after he'd disappeared, Sorbin stared after him. He didn't know if the male's claims were a prevalent thought in the clutch. He wasn't even certain who he could ask to find out.

"Hey, Sorbin."

Sorbin barely registered Jimmy's greeting, but his touch to the arm drew his attention. He turned and spotted the chieftain's human mate standing to the left. His head was cocked to the side, and his eyes were narrowed.

"Everything okay?" Jimmy asked. He glanced toward the exit Sorbin had been staring after. "You waiting for Rundin to come back or something?"

Shaking his head while trying to clear his thoughts, Sorbin forced a smile. "Uh, no. No." He indicated the table he'd been heading toward before being interrupted by . . . Rundin? Sorbin wasn't certain. "Ended up working a little longer in the office than planned, so I missed Destrawn coming out of roost." As Jimmy fell into step beside him, Sorbin admitted, "He said to meet him here."

Jimmy nodded, taking a seat beside him. "And you're not hungry?" He chuckled as he, too, placed a glass of wine on the table—his a blush pink. "I hear ya. With how early it gets dark this time of year, I need at least another couple of hours before I'm ready for a meal."

Sorbin nodded absently as he took a sip of his wine. As he rested his glass on the table, he noticed Jimmy eyeing him speculatively. Deciding to bite the bullet, Sorbin forced a smile.

"Penny for your thoughts?"

Snickering, Jimmy shook his head. "I was gonna offer you the same." His smile faded. "Don't take what Rundin said to heart. There's a reason he's a little . . . upset . . . about you and Destrawn getting together."

Spinning his wine glass absently, Sorbin asked, "Why?"

Jimmy grimaced while admitting, "Rundin has had a thing for Destrawn for a while. I guess, well—" He took a sip of his wine, his expression turning a little vacant. "The smaller gargoyles here really had a tough time, and Destrawn showed him kindness. Rundin kinda . . . latched onto that."

"Were they lovers?"

Sorbin wanted to take the question back as soon as the words were out of his mouth. He hadn't been a saint, after all.

Still, Sorbin couldn't help but wonder. While Destrawn had claimed he didn't have any close friends, that didn't mean he hadn't had lovers.

To Sorbin's relief, Jimmy immediately began shaking his head. "No. No way. Destrawn is way too honorable for that," the little human assured. "He and Rundin were *not* lovers, although Rundin would have been happy to change that."

Even as relief flooded Sorbin, he felt a measure of jealousy, too. The little gargoyle was obviously after his beloved. That knowledge caused his vampire nature to roar to life, urging him to discover a way to force his beloved to allow him to claim him, to prove to everyone that Destrawn was his and his alone.

"Why are you talking about Rundin?"

Sorbin jerked his head around, surprised to find Destrawn standing there holding a cup of coffee. He'd been so distracted by his thoughts that he hadn't even noticed his beloved's approach.

Jimmy didn't miss a beat, answering openly and honestly. "Rundin approached Sorbin and spouted out some not so nice things since you've been together for four days and you haven't finished your bonding, yet."

Feeling the blood drain from his face, Sorbin jerked his focus to his wine glass. Obviously, Jimmy had heard more than he'd let on. Sorbin tightened his grip on the stemware, then forced himself to relax it again. His heart thudded wildly in his chest, and as he heard the chair next to his own scrape as Destrawn sat next to him, he feared what his beloved would say.

Never in a million years would Sorbin have said something like that to Destrawn. He could already scent the acrid tinge of his anger. The smell was beating out his beloved's normally heady fragrance.

"Thank you for telling me, Jimmy," Destrawn rumbled

softly, his voice tight.

Jimmy hummed. "Sure. You know you need to fix this, right?" Out of the corner of his eye, Sorbin watched the chieftain's mate lean forward and pin Destrawn with a firm look. The human's next words were spoken so softly that, if Sorbin hadn't been a vampire, he wouldn't have heard them. "Destrawn, you really need to fix this. Hole up until your bond is complete. Okay? A leader of the clutch refusing to bond? Well." Jimmy cleared his throat and muttered, "That doesn't say much for our acceptance of Fate's blessings, does it?"

Destrawn groaned softly. "I'm sorry, Jimmy," he muttered. "Please know that's not what's going on here."

"I figured as much." Jimmy patted Destrawn's hand. "I'll let Kinsey and the rest of the inner circle know that if they need something, it'll have to be kept to the confines of your rooms."

Then Jimmy's chair scraped as he rose from his seat.

A few seconds later, they were alone, and Sorbin had no idea what to say.

When Destrawn's warm hand slid across his cheek, Sorbin jolted a bit. His gargoyle froze, then finished the move. With a bit of gentle pressure, his beloved urged Sorbin to meet his gaze.

Destrawn's gray eyes held a wealth of concern, and his brow ridges were drawn. "Tell me what Rundin said that upset you so." His lips curved into a wry smile. "And why our chieftain's mate is suddenly chastising me?"

Sorbin closed his eyes for a second. Then he inhaled deeply and leaned back in his chair, pulling away from Destrawn. He saw his beloved frown at the move, but he ignored it in favor of taking a sip of his wine so he could put together a response.

"First," Sorbin began. "I'm sorry for what I said on the phone." He kept his voice low, doing his best to keep their private matters just that — private. "Yes, I want to claim you, but I can be patient."

Dipping his chin in a nod, Destrawn told him, "You don't need to apologize for telling me your thoughts. If we were properly bonded, we'd feel each other through the vampire bond, anyway. I'm the one struggling." He reached over and gripped Sorbin's hand, squeezing lightly. "Now, answer my question about Rundin."

Sorbin squinted a little as he met Destrawn's gaze. "After Jimmy's explanation, I understand that he was speaking out of jealousy. He'll get over it eventually."

I hope.

Destrawn growled softly as he leaned closer. "Please answer my question, mate."

Clearing his throat, Sorbin nodded. "Okay. He's under the idea that I'm holding some kind of blackmail over you, and that's why you're claiming me as your mate. He told me to go back to my coven and leave you alone."

Narrowing his eyes, Destrawn grumbled, "Coming between fated mates, for any reason, is a punishable offense. Why would he do that?"

"He doesn't believe we're fated mates."

"Why, when I already presented you as such before the clutch?"

Sorbin knew he could only give one answer. "Because he doesn't believe we're fated" — after a second of hesitation, he finished — "because you won't let me claim you."

Growling under his breath, Destrawn rose from his seat. He held out his hand, palm up. "Come on, my mate," he urged, wiggling his fingers. "The rest of our conversation needs to be done in private."

While uncertain what else needed to be said that they hadn't already shared, Sorbin still took his beloved's hand and followed him from the dining hall.

CHAPTER NINE

Destrawn seethed with a mixture of anger, embarrassment, and shame. If this situation had happened to any other gargoyle, he would have offered the struggling gargoyle some simple advice.

This is your mate. It will be different. Trust in Fate and the mate-pull.

He wasn't taking his own advice.

As Destrawn guided Sorbin back to their suite, his mate asked, "Do you mind telling me what kindness you offered Rundin?"

Destrawn grimaced, but he knew he needed to admit the truth. "I complained about a crick in my neck one evening, and Rundin offered to give me a massage," he explained. Lifting his free hand to his neck as if a phantom memory caused stiffness, he explained, "I praised Rundin on his skills, and I advised him to take online masseuse courses. I figured learning something for himself would boost his confidence, you know?"

Too bad it'd worked a little too well.

"Anyway, he began using me as a guinea pig, and I didn't mind. Hell, he was good at it." Reaching their suite and leading the way inside, Destrawn admitted, "Before meeting you, sometimes when I woke from roost, I was sore in my upper back and neck." Scoffing, he admitted, "I think it was tension from my job or memories or past. I don't know and don't give a shit because now that I have you, I don't experience that." With a smile and shake of his head, he continued, "Anyway,

I enjoyed his help. It wasn't until recently, about a week before I headed to your coven, that I began to scent his arousal
and realized he was getting the wrong idea." He paused in
the front room and rested his hands on Sorbin's shoulders,
massaging lightly as he stared into his mate's pale blue eyes.
"Please know, even before meeting you, I had no intention of
starting anything with Rundin." Grimacing, knowing he had
to explain why, Destrawn admitted, "Before you, I only took
part in friend-with-benefits relationships, but that was all at
my past coven." Shrugging, he told him, "I hadn't bothered
to find a lover since coming here over a year ago."

For a long moment, Sorbin stared up at him. His blue-eyed
gaze roved over Destrawn's face. His scent gave nothing
away, and neither did his expression.

Finally, Sorbin smiled faintly. "You were trying to do a
good thing." He smirked then as his tone took on just a hint
of amusement. "And you might have used his interest in massage to your own advantage, too. Nothing wrong with that. It
wasn't as if you led him on."

Destrawn felt the tension ease from his shoulders. "Thank
you for understanding." To Destrawn's disappointment,
Sorbin nodded, but his expression still appeared troubled.
"Please tell me what you're thinking?"

*Gods, not being able to prod his mind a little with that vampire
link thingy really sucks.*

I could have it, though. I just need to get my head out of my ass.

"Exactly how many times do you think you need to suck
me off before you go through molt?"

Sorbin's question caused Destrawn's lips to part in surprise. He snapped them closed just as quickly. "Is that what
you think I'm trying to do?" he asked gruffly, his mind reeling.

Sorbin's shoulders lifted under Destrawn's hands as his
mate shrugged. "Yes," he admitted, obviously being brutally
honest. "We haven't talked about me claiming you since that

first time. What am I supposed to think?"

Growling, Destrawn turned away from Sorbin. He paced halfway across the room. Staring at the far wall, he scratched at his scalp with his claws.

"Hey," Sorbin crooned, resting his hand on Destrawn's bicep. "I told you I was willing to wait until you're ready, and I meant it." Destrawn felt Sorbin massage his muscle lightly. "That's not going to change just because of Rundin's accusations or Jimmy's warnings."

When Destrawn felt Sorbin tug at his arm, he turned to face him. The patient, understanding look on his mate's face caused his breath to catch. His deep blue eyes and the affectionate gleam there sent a fissure of heat through his gut, just as it always did.

Despite the serious conversation, Destrawn felt his blood heat and flow south . . . same as always around Sorbin.

"The problem is," Destrawn began slowly. "I want to submit to you." Grimacing, he told him, "I just fear that I'll be so tense through the whole thing neither one of us will end up enjoying it."

Sorbin's eyes narrowed as he cocked his head. "Think you'll be too tense, huh?" he murmured softly.

Destrawn nodded. "I like to be in control."

Cocking his head, Sorbin appeared contemplative. His expression turned vacant. He even slowly panned his gaze around the room as if he wasn't really seeing it.

"Relaxed and in control," Sorbin whispered, clearly thinking over something.

Confused, Destrawn waited for his mate to work through whatever was rattling around in his mind.

Finally, Sorbin blinked once. Then he snapped his focus back to Destrawn. His attention roved over him from top to bottom and back again before meeting his gaze.

"How about you stay in charge of everything while I make

you super relaxed." As Sorbin spoke, a growl entered his voice. "Relaxed and needy. When you can think of nothing but my cock in your ass, you can take it. Your speed." Narrowing his eyes, the blue of his irises darkened as the scent of his arousal began to tease Destrawn's nostrils. "Will you let me take care of you for a change?"

Destrawn hesitated only an instant before he nodded. He wanted to be connected to his vampire. He just had to figure out how to get out of his own way.

If Sorbin can help me do that, I'll do whatever he wants.

This time, it was Destrawn who took Sorbin's held out hand. He followed his lover into their bedroom. Even as nerves caused his gut to clench — as well as his ass — Destrawn felt a measure of anticipation, too.

Sorbin had been right that night they'd first met. As paranormals, their sex drives were heightened, just like their other senses. When they found their other half, that need to couple, to connect, damn near skyrocketed.

"Let's get this off of you, Dee," Sorbin crooned, reaching for the stays of his loincloth. "Time to get us both comfortable."

With a quick tug and yank, Sorbin had Destrawn's loincloth free of him and falling to the floor. His vampire rested his palms on his torso, rubbing down to his abdominals. When Sorbin wrapped one hand around his soft cock while cradling his balls with the other, Destrawn sucked in a breath.

Pleasure flooded his veins, quickly flowing south. It only took a few slow, tight, gut-clenching tugs of Sorbin's lightly-calloused hand to bring him to full mast. Unable to help himself, Destrawn spread his legs a little, giving his mate more room to hold his balls.

Destrawn stared at where Sorbin played with his genitals, and he couldn't help rocking into his touch.

When Sorbin eased the hand holding his ball sack backward, Destrawn couldn't help but tense.

Sorbin immediately stopped . . . everything.

Groaning, Destrawn tipped his head back. "Sorry," he grumbled, upset with himself and his instinctual response. "I—" He shook his head.

"Don't apologize for your natural responses, Destrawn," Sorbin countered. "We'll get to where we need to go." With a smile, he yanked his polo shirt over his head. As Sorbin began working on his jeans, he added, "Even if that means we don't reach our destination this time around."

Even though Destrawn wanted to deny Sorbin's words, to claim that he would let his mate take him, he knew he couldn't promise that.

Resigning to that fact, Destrawn took the opportunity to admire his vampire mate. The man's body was lean and toned, full of sinewy strength. His shaggy, sandy-blond hair hung around his face and sometimes in his eyes, giving him a sultry mischievous look when he peered at Destrawn through his lashes.

"Will you lie down on the bed, Destrawn?" Sorbin asked softly as he opened the nightstand drawer. "On your stomach in the middle? Hands folded under your head if that's the most comfortable."

Even as Destrawn moved to the bed, he couldn't help but ask, "What are you going to do?"

Pulling something from the drawer, Sorbin held up a bottle as he waggled his eyebrows. "Give you a massage."

Destrawn nodded slowly as he climbed onto the bed, reading the label that said hand lotion. "Okay." As he relaxed on his belly, he did his best to ignore the way his cock had softened to half-mast with his nerves. Something else occurred to him. "Um." Spreading his arms, Destrawn rested his hands on either side of his head. "You know this isn't a competition with Rundin, right?"

Sorbin snarled, showing off his fangs. Curling his lips, he

snapped, "Thoughts of another man, no matter who, has no place in our bedroom."

Acceptably chastised, Destrawn quickly nodded. "My apologies, my mate."

Sighing, Sorbin climbed onto the bed, kneeling beside his hip. "Sorry, I—" His vampire stopped and grimaced. His expression turned troubled. "Please tell me he didn't massage your wings."

"Hell, no!" Destrawn bellowed, a new tension rolling through him. "Never. That's taboo without permission, regardless of the situation. Every gargoyle knows that."

Bowing his head, Sorbin let out a deep sigh. When he lifted his head, a chagrined smile teased at the corners of his lips. "Sorry. Just . . . had to control a flood of jealousy there. Just at the idea. I—" He cut himself off, ceasing his nonsensical partial sentences. Meeting Destrawn's gaze, Sorbin asked, "Forgive me?"

Destrawn smiled. "You're a vampire, Sorbin. How would you know?" He shrugged. "There's nothing to forgive." Then he told him seriously. "From here on out, no concerns of what happened in the past with other men . . . from either of us. Our lives are with each other now. Forever."

Sorbin nodded. "Agreed. Forever."

As Destrawn relaxed again, eyeing Sorbin out of the corner of his eye, he tried to keep those words at the forefront of his mind.

This is my mate. He'll never do anything but please me. No other men in my bed, even in my memories, ever again.

Destrawn knew it was easier said than done, and he had never felt so damn grateful that Sorbin seemed to understand that, too.

Then Sorbin tossed a tube of lube on the bed on Destrawn's other side before opening the lotion and squirting a handful onto his palm. Sorbin placed that next to the lube. Then he rubbed his hands together, coating his fingers.

Unable to help himself, Destrawn glanced toward the discarded items.

Sorbin's hand on his lower back brought Destrawn's focus back to his mate. His vampire rubbed up and down lightly, getting him acclimated to his touch in this position. He smiled and winked.

"That's just in case we get that far," Sorbin assured.

Even as Destrawn nodded, he prayed to whatever gods cared to listen that he could pull that off. He wanted to give his vampire what he needed. Plus, he really wanted to go through molt. He wanted to be with his mate day and night, only turning to stone and roosting when he chose.

"All right," Sorbin crooned softly, beginning to move his hand, which was quickly joined by the second. "I'll admit it's been a while since I've given a massage, but with your erogenous zones, that kind of relaxation isn't really what I'm going for."

Destrawn was about to ask Sorbin what he meant. Then his mate rubbed up his spine to tease around where his wings met his shoulder blades, and all questions evaporated from his mind. Tingles erupted along his appendages, and pleasure swept through his body, warming him from the inside out.

Humming, Destrawn scraped his claws over the top of the comforter as he fought his desire to press into Sorbin's teasing touches. He shivered when his lover rubbed over his back's sides, skimming under his wings, teasing them. Then he returned to where they connected to his back, and he gripped the top bone, rubbing up along them.

Destrawn groaned and spread his wings wider, the move beyond his control. His stomach clenched, and when Sorbin rubbed back down his top bone, he couldn't stop his need to arch a bit, pushing into the sensation. Closing his eyes, Destrawn gave himself over to the delicious tingles spreading over his body, created by the slow, sensual move of his mate's hands. Sorbin continued to touch, on and on, and Destrawn lost track of time, his senses drowning. While the buzz of arousal hummed through his blood, his beloved seemed to know just when to back off to keep him from becoming too overwhelmed with need.

When Sorbin pulled his hands away, Destrawn whimpered, unable to control the noise of distress and disappointment.

"Easy, my beloved," Sorbin purred. "I'm just getting more lotion."

In his bliss-drunk state, Destrawn could barely nod. He heard the snick of the container, then a squelching noise and a click. The light odor of the lotion flooded the air anew.

"Spread your legs for me, Dee," Sorbin encouraged, sliding one hand between them and gripping his inner thigh. "I wanna get between them so I can get more leverage."

With his mind floating pleasantly, Destrawn would have agreed to damn near anything. He spread his legs and felt the bed jostle. The heat of his mate's thighs pressing against the sensitive inner flesh of his own registered, but he couldn't find it in himself to be alarmed.

Sorbin once again placed his hands on his back, and Destrawn sighed. His anticipation filled him, and he couldn't wait for more wing-petting. While he'd learned that his wings were an erogenous zone centuries before, never had someone petting them felt as Sorbin's hands on him did. His mind sang with the bliss of it, and he never wanted the sizzling sensations to stop.

Except, even as Sorbin lifted one hand and began rubbing over his wings again, he slid his other hand down . . . down.

When Sorbin stroked a finger along each side of the dock of his tail, Destrawn sucked in a surprised breath.

"Easy, Dee," Sorbin crooned. "Just exploring."

Destrawn knew Sorbin had misunderstood his reaction.

He couldn't remember anyone touching his dock . . . ever. The spark that the touch elicited . . . it had gone straight to his balls.

Opening his eyes, Destrawn stared blindly at the wall. He parted his lips, trying to figure out how to speak, how to express what he suddenly wanted with everything in him.

Except, Sorbin seemed to be one step ahead of him. His mate rubbed two fingers down the base of his tail with the other two on either side, teasing his ass cheeks. Unable to stop it even if he'd tried, his tail lifted, as if seeking more touches all on its own.

Sorbin didn't disappoint. He did it again . . . and again.

As Sorbin continued to stroke him, Destrawn's gut clenched. His tail twitched. Even his cock began to twitch, leaking into the comforter.

Then Sorbin wrapped his hand around his tail and squeezed, sliding his hand down as if he were jacking his prick.

Fire shot up Destrawn's spine. His entire groin goose bumped. But that wasn't the most shocking thing. He felt his chute muscles loosen, and he suddenly ached to feel something slide inside him.

Destrawn moaned with need as sweat popped out on his brow. "Please," he begged, needing more. "Please, my mate."

Out of his mind with need, Destrawn did something he'd never done for another. He slid his knees under him and spread his legs, presenting himself. Digging his claws into the comforter, ignoring the rip of fabric, Destrawn lifted his tail higher and arched, all while pleading for more, for his lover to do something, to do . . . anything.

CHAPTER TEN

H*oly fucking shit!*
Sorbin couldn't believe Destrawn's responses. If his beloved wasn't babbling his begging, coupled with his trembling body, he would have believed his senses were muddled. No way in hell would he have thought a little tail play would cause such a reaction in his gargoyle.

Except, Destrawn appeared to be especially sensitive along his dock and first foot and a half of the appendage. His lover practically vibrated each time he gripped his dock and squeezed downward about twenty-four inches. The fact that his lover had begun to shred his comforter with his need hadn't escaped his notice, either.

Doing his best to keep up the pressure on Destrawn's tail, Sorbin grabbed the lube with one hand. He popped the cap and awkwardly poured some onto his fingers one-handed. Seeing as the blanket was ruined anyway, he didn't try to close it, instead just dropping it next to Destrawn's knee.

His gargoyle didn't even seem to notice, too caught up in his pleasure. When Sorbin teased at Destrawn's entrance with his fingertip, he received a response. It just wasn't the one he expected.

Destrawn arched his tail over his back, offering more room. He bent his back even more.

The look of debauched need presented before Sorbin nearly took his breath away. As he continued to work Destrawn's tail, he eased a finger deep into the gargoyle's rectum. His lover took it easily, so he pulled it out, then pushed in a second beside it. With that one, Sorbin found Destrawn's prostate, rubbing over it experimentally.

The howl that rocked the room would have put a wolf to shame. The ecstatic delight in the sounds erupting from his beloved caused Sorbin's own erection to jerk. His prick throbbed painfully, nearly tapping his stomach with how engorged he was.

The scent of his beloved's leaking pre-cum mixed with arousal perfumed the air, and Sorbin found it was beginning to get difficult to think. Refusing to entertain hurting his lover, he eased a third finger into him. Even that was swallowed with ease.

Shit. Shit. Shit.

Sorbin could feel his balls pull up, and he knew if he didn't get into Destrawn's silky ass damn fast, he would come untouched.

"D-Dee," Sorbin managed to start. "D-Do you—" His words ended on a groan when he felt Destrawn's heated chute muscles ripple along his embedded fingers. "Dee!"

"Yesssss," Destrawn snarled. Peering over his shoulder at him, Sorbin couldn't ever remember anyone looking at him with such stark, feral need . . . as if they would go right out of their skin if they didn't get what they craved. "Take me, my mate," Destrawn demanded, his voice so guttural, so raspy and low, that Sorbin had a hard time understanding. "Now!"

Sorbin understood that.

Lifting higher on his knees, Sorbin eased his fingers out of Destrawn's channel, doing his best to ignore his beloved's dismayed moan. He grabbed his own dick and greased himself up as swiftly as possible. Then Sorbin levered over Destrawn's larger body, using his hold on the male's tail to put him where he wanted him.

Then, with one hand on the mattress by Destrawn's shoulder, Sorbin crooned, "Push out," even as he gave his gargoyle's tail another tight stroke.

Sorbin probably hadn't needed to offer the advice. With so little effort, just a steady push, he plunged deep, *deep* into his gargoyle's body. Silky rippling heat enveloped him from tip to root.

By the time Sorbin bottomed out, his eyes had nearly rolled to the back of his head. He couldn't ever remember a more exquisite embrace. Maybe it was partly due to the fact that he usually wore a condom, seeing as he coupled with humans for their blood. Still, something told Sorbin that that wasn't it.

This is my beloved, the other half of my soul. This is the one being Fate created just for me.

Recalling their age differences, Sorbin had to smile.

Or I was made for him.

"Move."

Upon hearing the guttural, hissing command, Sorbin grinned. He'd told Destrawn that he would be in control, and hell would freeze over before he went back on his word. Sorbin did as he'd been bidden. He began to move.

Sorbin eased out of Destrawn's tight channel, gritting his teeth to keep from shooting. The hot squeeze along his length took his breath away. His balls were drawing so tight, and his fangs ached in a way he'd never before experienced.

Except, Sorbin refused to finish before pleasing Destrawn. He planned for his gargoyle to want to repeat the experience. That meant getting him off . . . more than once.

Besides, call him a bastard, but it was a matter of pride.

Sorbin finally released Destrawn's tail in favor of sliding his hand under him. Before his beloved could finish his groan of dismay — *gods, gonna tease his tail often* — he grabbed his beloved's dick. At the same time, Sorbin thrust back into his gargoyle, pegging his gland.

To Sorbin's satisfaction, Destrawn's groan of discontent morphed into a hiss of pure delight. When he began jacking his gargoyle's huge erection, his gargoyle growled. Then he felt the way Destrawn's hips shimmied under him, and he realized what his lover wanted.

He needs control.

Stilling his own hips was the hardest damn thing Sorbin had ever done in his life, but he accomplished it. He held steady as he hissed, "Do it. Take what you need. My body is for your pleasure."

That was all Destrawn must have needed to hear. His gargoyle began moving. He lifted his hips, slamming up onto Sorbin's dick. Then he jerked forward, thrusting his dick through the tunnel of Sorbin's fingers.

Sorbin moaned as Destrawn did that again, over and over. His body trembled with his need to move, but he didn't. Instead, he let Destrawn have all the control.

"C-Close," Sorbin warned as the tingle behind his spine began to intensify. A tremble worked through him, and he fought to keep his orgasm at bay.

To Sorbin's ever-loving relief, Destrawn thrust into his fist one last time and stilled. He felt the dick in his hand pulse and smelled the delicious aroma of his seed. Unable to help himself, Sorbin buried his prick deep inside his lover and stilled, pouring his fluid into his beloved.

With his heart pounding in his chest, Sorbin didn't think he would be able to move for a while. Except, there was something . . . something he was missing. Acting on instinct, Sorbin wrapped his arm around Destrawn's torso. He twisted them awkwardly, which allowed him to reach the man's neck.

Sorbin sank his fangs deep into Destrawn's hide. His beloved's life-giving fluid flowed around his teeth, and he sucked hard, filling his mouth with even more. He swallowed, then moaned at the delectable flavor.

More, his mind screamed.

Giving in, Sorbin drank deeply of his beloved. He felt the gargoyle shudder beneath him. His lover's moans were music to his ears. The scents of seed and sweat flooded his senses in the best possible way.

With his thirst abated, Sorbin regained control. He eased his fangs free, then sealed the twin wounds. Seeing them scar, he smiled.

"Gods," Sorbin mumbled.

Destrawn groaned roughly. He turned his head, revealing his eyes were at half-mast. "I—" Pausing, he licked his lips, then swallowed. "I—" Destrawn's brow ridges furrowed. "W-Wow. N-Never."

Sorbin heard the confusion in Destrawn's sluggish and slurred voice. Needing to soothe, he rubbed down his gargoyle's side, then back up again. Nuzzling at Destrawn's neck, he suddenly wished he had the ability to trill.

Well, I can't do that, but I can do something similar.

Ever-so-carefully, Sorbin eased out of Destrawn's chute. He gritted his teeth at the sensation of his beloved's hot chute releasing his over-sensitized flesh. Then Sorbin began to gently skim the fingertips of one hand over one of Destrawn's wings while using his other hand to encourage him to move to his left onto his side.

Sorbin urged Destrawn all the way onto his back. Then he crawled up to sprawl halfway across his chest. To his pleasure, Destrawn kept his far side wing draped partially over his shoulder, allowing Sorbin to continue to pet it, telling him his gargoyle obviously needed the comfort.

For a long moment, they just lay there, relishing in the afterglow.

Finally, Sorbin decided to break the silence. "You feeling okay, my beloved?" he asked softly.

"More than," Destrawn replied before letting out a raspy chuckle. "Wow." Tipping his head down, he pecked a kiss to Sorbin's lips. Then his lips curved into a wide, sated smile. "How the fuck did you do that?"

Sorbin took a second to peer into Destrawn's deep gray eyes. His beloved stared at him with disbelief and wonder.

He couldn't help but imagine how long it'd been for the gargoyle to feel that way.

Upon seeing Destrawn lift one brow ridge to punctuate his question, Sorbin hummed. "Well," he began slowly. "I, um—" He paused and cleared his throat. After a quick swallow, Sorbin admitted, "I spotted Basques and Dloben in the hall once. Basques was, um, teasing the dock of Dloben's tail and . . . well, Dloben was enjoying it. A lot." Rubbing the back of his neck, Sorbin admitted, "I could smell it, so I got out of there before anything happened or anything, but it was easy to see where it was leading to."

Chuckling softly, Destrawn wrapped his arms around Sorbin's torso and clutched him close. "Thank you, my mate." He scoffed softly, his eyes wide and still slightly dilated. "Never had anyone touch my tail. Could never have guessed."

Unable to help himself, Sorbin asked hesitantly, "Not even, um—" He snapped his mouth shut, recalling that they'd promised not to discuss past men when in their bed.

Destrawn still must have understood. "No," he confirmed quietly. His arms tightened around Sorbin. "His lessons were all about his own pleasure."

Sorbin nodded against Destrawn's shoulder, then relaxed, willing to let the matter lie.

Turning his head, Destrawn nuzzled the top of Sorbin's head. "I'm gonna ask you to do that again," he whispered huskily. "Many, many times." Destrawn sighed. "What you did to me, my mate. Never had anyone pleasure me the way you did."

With his heart thrilling in his chest for a whole new reason, Sorbin tipped his head up and smiled at Destrawn. "Any time you want, my beloved. Any time."

Grinning, Destrawn took Sorbin's mouth in a long, languorous kiss.

Watching Destrawn go through molt had been one of the hardest experiences of Sorbin's life. His instincts had been to care for and help his gargoyle, but there was very little he could do. He'd known the experience would be painful to the male, changing into a human form for the first time, but the groans, the gritted teeth, and the tension that pervaded his lover told him just how much agony Destrawn fought through.

Destrawn told Sorbin that the stroking of his skin helped, but in his opinion, it hadn't been enough. Fortunately, the first change was the only one that would hurt. In the future, it would be similar to what a shifter felt when changing—the sensation of a really good stretch after sitting for too long.

Pleased it was over, Sorbin helped a wrung out Destrawn into the shower. As he washed the sweat from his beloved's body, he marveled at the changes.

His gargoyle's dark-green mottled hide had bronzed out to a rich copper color. He'd lost about four inches of height, leaving him at six-foot-six. Between his black hair and deep gray eyes, he appeared to be a muscular Native American.

"What do you think?" Destrawn asked softly as he stood for Sorbin's ministrations.

Sorbin arched a brow as he smoothed the loofah down Destrawn's side, then up his back. "What do you mean? Think about what?"

Destrawn peered over his shoulder at him, a wan smile curving his lips. "Do I look okay?"

"You're hot as hell," Sorbin answered honestly. "I'm going to have to beat the competition off with a stick."

Of course, as a paranormal, he would have thought Destrawn attractive regardless of what he looked like. He didn't mention that, though. Instead, Sorbin rubbed his soapy empty hand over Destrawn's other side while reaching around to smooth the washcloth over his lover's abdominals.

"You'll never have competition for my attention, Sorbin," Destrawn replied. He turned and leaned his back against the wall. Taking the cloth from Sorbin's hand, he wrapped his other one around Sorbin's waist and hauled him against him. "You're the only one I'll ever want or need."

Sorbin knew that, so he said so. Growling softly, he added, "You know I feel the same about you, and it's not just because you're my beloved."

"Sure it is," Destrawn countered with a shrug. He smirked down at him, a warm gleam in his eye. "And there's nothing wrong with that. Fate brought us together, and together we'll stay."

Nodding, understanding, Sorbin replied, "Then let's do what we can to secure our people's safety." He wrapped his arms around Destrawn's neck and pressed his body against his wet, naked lover. "Now that you have a human form, why don't we explore the town? I have an idea."

Destrawn's lips tightened, and his eyes narrowed. "Are you trying to use your wiles to get your way?" Resting his hands on Sorbin's hips, he widened his legs to lower his stance.

Feeling Destrawn's hardening prick align with his own thickening dick, Sorbin hummed. "If I'd planned to do that"—he hissed when his beloved began a slow rut—"I would have done it while petting your wings."

Growling softly, Destrawn muttered, "Good point." He lowered his head. Just before capturing Sorbin's lips, he whispered, "Whatever your idea is, we'll work it out."

Sorbin knew that wasn't a yes, but with his wet, naked beloved holding him, touching him, ravishing him with hands and mouth, he decided to worry about it later.

Chapter Eleven

Destrawn wasn't entirely certain how Sorbin had convinced him this was a good idea.

Oh, right. After a shower blowjob, my brain is mush.

For the first time in centuries, Destrawn felt a thick case of nerves. He'd never walked among humans before. Even though he knew he looked like one of them, he still felt the hairs on his neck stand on end.

"Relax," Sorbin crooned, reaching out and taking his hand and threading their fingers together. "We're supposed to be sightseeing, exploring this little tourist town," he reminded Destrawn. "Stop looking as if everyone is out to get us."

"It is . . . difficult," Destrawn admitted, looking around at all the small stores that lined Main Street of Lake Point. "I've never . . ."

"I know, Dee," Sorbin responded when Destrawn allowed his words to trail off. He squeezed his fingers. Keeping his voice low, Sorbin told him, "You'll get used to it. I look forward to sharing the best aspects of the human world with you."

Destrawn smiled down at Sorbin. His heart swelled with warmth for the man strolling beside him. After getting a smile in return, he returned his attention to the area.

While Destrawn had learned to drive a vehicle decades before, simply because he'd been interested, the variety available these days blew his mind. He'd heard the excitement in the voices of humans in his old clutch when they discussed them, but he didn't understand it. Destrawn saw them as a tool — something to help get a job done or to get someone from point A to B.

Humans, however, saw them as a status symbol.

As Destrawn saw an SUV style vehicle with a *BMW* logo on the front pull into a slanted parking space, he wondered if it was better or worse than the one the vampires had used to help Sorbin move.

Destrawn was about to dismiss the notion when he saw who was getting out of it. He recognized the picture of the man who'd been driving as a hunter known as Vynce Walsh. The second man was a stranger, but the woman sliding from the passenger seat was none other than Alexa Milligan.

Turning to face the window of the small store they'd been passing, Destrawn tried out the mind-link he and Sorbin had discovered that morning.

Use the window glass to check out the trio down the street to the left.

Sorbin squeezed Destrawn's hand back and appeared to do it.

A second later, Destrawn heard Sorbin's voice in his head. He barely resisted the urge to flinch. Hearing another in his mind was still such a new experience, but he hoped to get used to it soon.

Damn. That's Alexa Milligan and Reginald, the guy posing as her husband at the bed and breakfast, but he's actually her brother. Don't know what that's all about. The driver is Vynce Walsh. They're dressed for hiking.

Destrawn realized Sorbin was right. *Wonder where they're going . . . after lunch.* He noticed the trio enter a café with signs offering pastries, hot and cold sandwiches, and the best potato salad in Lake Point.

Huh. Wonder if that's actually true.

What's true?

Realizing he'd inadvertently projected his last thought, Destrawn rolled his eyes. Then he pointed at the sign. "Do you think they really have the best potato salad in town?"

Sorbin winked. "You want to check?" Turning in that direction, he added, "It would give us a chance to eavesdrop on their conversation."

Destrawn nodded. "I like that idea."

With a hand on Sorbin's lower back, Destrawn walked with his mate down the sidewalk. He reached past his vampire and opened the door for him. That earned him an amused smile from his lover, so he just shrugged.

Sorbin chuckled softly as he led the way to the counter.

Reading the menu, Destrawn checked out his options. He chose a hot ham and Swiss on a sourdough roll. With it, he chose a fruit custard cup, the potato salad, and a lemonade.

"What about for you, sir?" the young woman behind the counter smiled shyly at Sorbin. She leaned forward on her arm, which showed off the tops of her tits in her too low shirt.

Good grief.

Destrawn wanted to snarl at her, since she was clearly coming onto his man.

Can't she see that I have my hand on his back?

"I'll go with the Rueben on sourdough bread with French fries, the biggest lemon bar you have back there, and a medium soda."

"You got it," she replied, straightening and typing in their order. "I love the lemon bars, too. You can't go wrong with them."

After she restated the order, Destrawn whipped out his credit card before Sorbin could and paid for them both. She cast a speculative glance between them, and Destrawn hoped that got the message across. It didn't.

When she pulled the lemon bar out of the display case, she once more gave Sorbin a flirty look while saying, "Be sure to come on back up here and tell me what you think when you're done."

Sorbin offered her a smile and small nod as he took it.

"Thank you."

After taking his bottle of lemonade, Destrawn took Sorbin's hand and led him away from the counter. He chose a table on the far side of the deli, since being a paranormal, they wouldn't have any trouble eavesdropping even from a distance. Plus, it was far away from the counter.

When they reached the table and Sorbin put down his pastry, the vampire chuckled softly. His blue eyes danced with mirth as he murmured, "Jealous isn't really a good look on you, handsome."

Destrawn growled under his breath. Upon seeing Sorbin's arched brow and smirk, he suddenly realized how ridiculous he was being. His ire dissolved as he shook his head.

"My apologies, my m—my love." Destrawn barely caught himself in time. No way did he want to use the term mate anywhere near hunters. "Our relationship is so new, and I—" Destrawn shrugged, uncertain how to finish that sentence.

Sorbin squeezed Destrawn's shoulder as he moved past him. "I'm all yours, Dee," he assured. "You know that."

After squeezing Sorbin's hand before his vampire pulled it away, Destrawn nodded. He did know it. Except, as a newly bonded couple, he was still getting a hold of his possessive instincts.

Cracking open his bottle of lemonade, Destrawn watched Sorbin cross to the soda machine. He pulled a medium-sized cardboard cup from the dispenser, then made a selection. As Sorbin filled his cup, Reginald crossed the deli to the machine.

Sorbin was just placing his lid on his drink when Reginald reached the area. As his vampire moved around where the man was getting his own cup to return to the table, Reginald stuck out his elbow and nailed him in the back. The human took a step toward the dispensers, as if that were the reason for the collision, doing a piss-pour job of hiding the fact that it wasn't a random accident.

Probably on instinct, Sorbin narrowed his eyes and frowned at the man. "Watch it," he warned.

The human scoffed. As he had an inch on Sorbin's six-foot-one frame and was quite a bit broader, he curled his lip and stared down his nose at Sorbin. "Naw, it's you who's gotta watch where you're goin', faggot."

The man glanced Destrawn's way as if he intended to say more. Then he must have registered just how large he was. Instead of saying more to Sorbin, he turned back to the machine to get his drink.

Even with his back to them, Destrawn still heard the guy mutter, "Damn cocksuckin' degenerates comin' out and tryin' to mix with good, regular folk."

Destrawn had been so caught up in eyeing the human hunter, it wasn't until Sorbin placed his drink on the table that he realized he'd returned. He lifted his gaze to his vampire as Sorbin leaned toward him. A wry smile curved his lips, and a gleam of amusement lit his blue eyes.

"At least we know he's an equal opportunity bigot," Sorbin whispered with amusement. "I'll get the food."

As Destrawn began to nod at the first part of what Sorbin stated, he processed his second comment. "Wait," he called, starting to rise.

With a laugh, Sorbin waved his hand and continued to the food pick-up area . . . where the young woman waited.

Destrawn took a deep breath, then let it out slowly. Keeping a sharp eye on the human hunter as well as his lover, who was checking over their order, he noticed the second Reginald drew near. His sensitive hearing easily made out the man's snide comment as he passed the pick-up area.

"You don't want to associate with the likes of him, darlin'," the human drawled, a mixture of innuendo and derision in his tone. "His proclivities don't make him good folk. Not good for your reputation, ya see." Then as he leaned on the glass, he added, "But if you're lookin' for a date to a New Year's party, I could pick ya up at ten. I'm sure my other plans will be wrapped up by then."

As much as Destrawn wanted to jump from his seat, stalk across the deli, and ram his fist into the human's face for his talk, he knew he couldn't. One, a normal human wouldn't have been able to hear the guy's words over the sound of the heater vent to his left. Also, he didn't think it would help his cover as a tourist or strengthen his relationship if he acted as if Sorbin couldn't handle himself.

To Destrawn's surprise, the woman behind the counter didn't bat an eyelash. In fact, she didn't even bother responding to the hunter. Instead, she grinned brightly at Sorbin, placed a hand over her chest, and sighed deeply.

"Story of my life," she said with a smile. With a wink while pointing toward Destrawn, she claimed, "Your man has good taste. You be sure he treats you right."

Sorbin picked up the tray of food as he chuckled. "Oh, he treats me very well." Then, with a wink of his own, he added, "And if he doesn't, I'll be sure to smack his ass."

She laughed and began heading back to the register.

The hunter's face turned beet red, realizing he'd been ignored. "Fuckers," he grumbled as he stalked back to the table with his drink.

After placing the tray on the table, Sorbin sat to Destrawn's left. "I bet staying seated was damn difficult," he murmured astutely while placing the food in front of them. Sorbin smiled warmly at Destrawn and stated, "Thank you."

Destrawn nodded. "You're welcome, and you're right."

"But we found out some interesting information," Sorbin claimed, grabbing the bottle of ketchup from the center of the table and pouring a dollop on his plate. "Don't you think?"

We had?

Destrawn made certain to keep that thought to himself as he re-ran the last few minutes of conversations in his head.

Frowning, he picked up his sandwich as one of the hunter's comments jumped out at him. Before taking a bite, Destrawn asked, "Do you mean his offer to pick up that girl at ten?"

Sorbin nodded as he swallowed his bite of Rueben. "Exactly," he replied softly, leaning toward Destrawn. "He thinks his plans will be wrapped up well before then, which means the attack will happen several hours prior to that."

Humming as he chewed, Destrawn smiled. He swallowed, then stated, "Well, then our New Year's Eve party isn't in danger, then is it?" Destrawn chuckled low in his throat as anticipation filled him. He couldn't wait to take care of whatever the hunters decided to throw at them in two days' time. "I look forward to handing that guy his ass." Picking up his fork to try the potato salad, Destrawn stated, "We should hurry. We need to get back to share what we've learned."

Sorbin chuckled before taking a swig of his soda. "We still have one more stop," he murmured, shaking his head.

Before Sorbin could continue, the woman began speaking, catching their attention. "I do hope you're right in that it'll take less than three hours," she stated, stabbing her fork into her salad leaves. "I have a buyer to meet at ten-thirty, and these are not the type of people you keep waiting." Before popping her fork into her mouth, she added haughtily, "Besides, fulfilling a buyer's order on time with exactly what they need is a matter of pride in my business."

Destrawn felt his blood go cold as he met Sorbin's gaze. His vampire's eyebrows were drawn, and a muscle ticked in his jaw.

"Don't worry, Alexa," Reginald assured, sitting back in his chair and tossing his napkin on his plate. "Everything will go according to plan. Without help from their friends, they're vulnerable."

"Stop talking about this here," Vynce ordered with a growl before glancing around the space.

As the human's gaze swept his way, Destrawn pointed at his potato salad and stated, "This is pretty good. Wanna try?"

Sorbin seemed to catch on quick, for he nodded and opened his mouth while leaning forward.

Destrawn feigned a chuckle as he scooped up a dollop. Then he leaned over and eased the tines between his vampire's parted lips. As his lover closed his mouth and he pulled it from between them, Destrawn felt heat erupt through his gut, and his dick twitched behind the fly of his jeans.

With the way Sorbin's nostrils flared, Destrawn knew his lover had scented his sudden spike in arousal.

Before either of them could address it, Vynce rose from his chair, issuing a disgusted grunt. "Let's go explore," he declared. "I'm done dealing with those fucking perverts." Then Vynce stalked out of the deli.

The others quickly followed him out of the restaurant, casting dirty looks their way. Destrawn answered them with a smirk.

The bell on the door hadn't even finished dingling when the young woman who'd been behind the counter arrived at their table. "I'm so sorry you had to deal with their bigotry," she stated. "Here. Have a chocolate torte on the house. They're simply to die for." Then she was gone again.

Destrawn picked up his fork, happy to accept the free dessert.

After leaving the deli, Destrawn turned them back toward their old pick-up truck. He slid behind the wheel while Sorbin climbed in on the other end of the bench seat. Destrawn fired up the truck and headed toward the west side of town.

"Which road is the bed and breakfast on again?" Destrawn asked, checking street signs.

"It's called Biddle Street," Sorbin told him, pointing. "It should be up here on the left."

Destrawn spotted it and headed that way. After only half a mile, the bed and breakfast appeared on the right. He parked in front of it and turned off the pick-up.

Sorbin patted Destrawn's arm and winked. "Let me do the talking."

Nodding, Destrawn acquiesced, since he knew his mate had plenty of experience dealing with humans.

Without knocking, Sorbin headed through the door marked *Office*. He stopped at the desk and rang the bell. Then he leaned against it nonchalantly, shoving his hands into his pockets with a small smile playing across his lips.

"Afternoon," an older man greeted as he shuffled through a door to the left. "What can I do for ya?" He glanced between them, then held up his hand. "I should tell ya I only have one room left, and it only has one bed in it."

Sorbin straightened. "I understand." Shrugging, he claimed, "It never hurts to ask."

Then, to Destrawn's confusion, Sorbin started moving toward the door.

After just a couple of steps, Sorbin stopped and turned, saying, "You wouldn't be able to recommend somewhere else, would you? We prefer patroning small businesses such as yourselves"—Sorbin waved toward the old man, as if he wouldn't get it without the movement—"but we'd really like to hike the area, so even a motel would do in a pinch."

The old man shook his head, resting his gnarled hands on the desk between them. "Sorry, young man. The only place I know with availability is the motel on the other side of town." Furrowing his brows, he added, "Got a big hiking convention in town for some retreat thing."

"Oh, yeah?" Sorbin stepped closer and prodded, "Do you know where they plan to be exploring? We don't want to get in their way."

Rubbing his chin, the human hummed. "Well, they mentioned it at some point, but my memory ain't what it used to be."

Sorbin's irises bled red as he urged, "I'm sure we can jog your memory." His voice turned soothing. "Think about what brought the subject up."

The man's expression turned a little vacant as he nodded. "Oh, yeah," he mumbled after a second. "They plan to explore the Waikita Falls trails over the next few days."

Destrawn grimaced, not liking the sound of that. Waikita Falls wasn't the closest trail system, but it was definitely the most remote.

At least now we know a direction.

CHAPTER TWELVE

Sorbin knew that Destrawn wasn't at all pleased that he had insisted on helping, but his aid was needed.

Whether my beloved wants to accept it or not.

According to Lathe, who was monitoring the all-of-three traffic cameras in Lake Point, Alexa, Vynce, and their men had left the bed and breakfast at eleven that morning. That would mean they could be there via hiking as early as two in the afternoon, meaning only a handful of gargoyles were awake—Chieftain Kinsey, Second Destrawn, Enforcer Biers, Trackers Lionad and Pendral, as well as Wandrin, who walked the perimeter.

Of those gargoyles, only one had a mate who would be useful in a fight, and that was Biers's lion shifter mate, Dyson.

Considering there were over thirty hunters heading their way, that meant they were facing over three-to-one odds. Sorbin was needed, and he planned to do whatever it took to keep his new home safe. He knew he could easily take out three humans, guns or not.

Just as Kinsey was going over their defenses and where everyone was supposed to be, Sorbin's phone beeped harshly. "That's the proximity alarm," he declared when every eye in the room turned toward him. Pulling up the feed that Sorbin had had installed to Lathe's specifications as soon as he'd moved in—he didn't know how the gargoyles had gotten along without cameras before then—he felt his face pale. "Unknown SUV approaching."

"The group only left their hotels ten minutes ago," Jimmy

pointed out from where he sat on Kinsey's lap. Even though the chieftain's mate wasn't going to fight, he'd still insisted on sitting in on the meeting. "There's no way that's a hunter from town."

Switching feeds, Sorbin watched the vehicle park near the mansion's expansive garage. Three doors opened. As he watched the men who emerged, relief filled him mixed with a healthy amount of confusion.

One of the guys, a light-brown-haired guy, stared directly toward the camera and, while grinning widely, gave two thumbs up. Then he moved to the back of the SUV to help the others. They pulled large, black duffel bags over their shoulders and started toward the front door.

"Who is it?" Kinsey asked, yanking Sorbin from his shock.

Sorbin jerked his head up and met the chieftain's gaze. Barking a laugh, he grinned. "It's my friends. Lathe, Vicon, and Donny."

"You trust them?" the chieftain asked.

Nodding, Sorbin replied, "With my life."

Kinsey fixed a gaze on Destrawn and arched a brow in silent question.

Sorbin wasn't offended that the chieftain wouldn't take his word alone. He was new to Kinsey, after all.

Destrawn smirked and nodded. "They're unique, but they're good men."

As the doorbell rang, Kinsey refocused on Sorbin and smiled. "Help is welcome."

Jumping to his feet, Sorbin exited the study. He knew Destrawn was following. After all, with a battle imminent, his beloved wasn't going to allow him far from his side.

Sorbin trotted down the stairs using vampire speed. The whoosh of wings told him Destrawn flew to keep up. Reaching the door, he threw it open.

Instantly, Sorbin found himself enveloped in a hug.

"Hey, man," Donny greeted enthusiastically. "No way you goin' into a fight without us." After a slap to his back, he released him and grabbed onto Destrawn to give him a hug, too, much to the gargoyle's shock, judging by his scent and expression. Donny ignored it completely, clapping him on the back while saying, "He smells well sexed-up, Dee. Glad you're keeping him happy."

While Lathe snickered, Vicon rested his hand on the back of Sorbin's neck. "What the hell were you thinking by not telling us when they were attacking?" His dark-haired friend glared at him. "If I weren't already about to bust some heads, I'd kick your ass."

Sorbin glanced around the group. "But the coven is being attacked at the same time."

Donny, who'd released Destrawn and was standing with his arms crossed, snorted and rolled his eyes. "Yeah, and over half of those enforcers and trackers aren't sleeping," he pointed out on a scoff.

Lathe slammed the front door closed and dropped the duffel bag he was carrying. Rubbing his left thigh, he asked, "There's no place we'd rather be." Then with a grin, the slender male asked, "So, where's this awesome security room you've been putting together for me?"

Snickering, Sorbin grabbed Lathe and dragged him into a quick hug. He released his shy friend just as swiftly. Then he grabbed Lathe's dropped duffel and threaded his fingers with Destrawn's.

"Come on," Sorbin beckoned. "We'll drop off your stuff in my room. Then we need to return to our meeting." As they started down the hallway toward the central staircase, Sorbin sobered and stated, "Thank you for coming."

That started another round of razzing from his buddies.

At half-past two, everyone was in position. The vampires

hid on the roof with their vision hazed — a vampire ability allowing them to read the flow of blood in a body, similar to seeing heat signatures — one looking in each direction . . . just in case. That way, they could easily spot anything moving in the extremely chilly afternoon air.

Sorbin peered to the west, which was the main direction they thought the hunters would come from. Even Lathe was on the roof, although he faced the driveway — what they thought was the least dangerous position. His buddy wasn't offended, especially since he also had a laptop by his side, so he could monitor not only their own systems but the ones in town that he'd hacked.

Sorbin could handle himself on a computer, but he was in no way at Lathe's level. When the other vampire had tried to explain to Kinsey some of what he was doing, the chieftain's eyes had begun to glaze over. Then the gargoyle had cleared his throat and told him to use his discretion before moving on to a new subject.

As they'd spread out on the roof, Lathe had softly asked, "Did I upset Chieftain Kinsey during the meeting?"

Grinning, Sorbin had shaken his head. "Naw. He's super laid-back. Nothing like that would upset him." When Lathe still didn't look convinced, Sorbin explained, "Kinsey just had no clue what you were talking about, so he's placing his trust in you to make the best choices possible."

"Up to me?" Lathe appeared taken aback. "Why?"

Sorbin shrugged. "This is gonna be your home now. These will be your people. Why not you?"

Lathe had rubbed the back of his neck and muttered, "Huh."

A growing heat signature caught Sorbin's attention. Taking in the circulation of the blood in the form moving toward the mansion, he easily recognized it as a human. He panned left and right slowly, searching for more.

Once Sorbin felt certain he'd pegged everyone close enough for him to see, he tapped his com button. "This is Sorbin. Five slipping in from the west. Two near Biers's position."

For the sake of ease in communication, the chieftain had dropped the use of titles.

"Another is one hundred yards to Kinsey's left," Sorbin continued. His heart thudded as he finished, "Last two clustered fifty feet and closing to the right of Destrawn."

After Sorbin finished, three hulking red forms began carefully moving through the treetops, getting into position to take out all five in as swift a succession as possible.

"I have three coming in from the east." Vicon's deep voice came through the line. "Two are heading toward the back garden entrance where Dyson will be able to engage."

Dyson had chosen to take on the hunters in lion form, so he'd been positioned in and around the back garden. Lathe had done an amazing job of figuring out how to affix a communication device to the shifter's feline head.

"Another six to the south," Donny told everyone. "Seriously? Why are they clustering like that?" Then he snorted. "Oh. These must be the decoys. Lame. They stopped twenty-five yards to the left of Lionad's position. Can you move to assist, Wandrin? You're closest."

Instead of a verbal answer, a clicking noise came through the line once, indicating that the gargoyle male had acknowledged the request and would move into position. If Wandrin had had a problem with the order, he would have clicked twice. They'd decided on no verbal communication unless completely necessary by those in the field, since voices carried so easily across the snow.

"Hmm, I see more forms appearing behind my first wave," Sorbin told everyone. With almost thirty hunters to account for, he knew at least half had to have been hanging back, so it wasn't a surprise. "There's six here."

"Another five just showed up in my direction," Vicon claimed. "Pendral should move in to assist Dyson."

Another click came through the line.

"Huh," Donny grunted. "I only see two back-up here. Aren't we missing at least three? Maybe four?"

"Um, well, they may be in the *BMW* coming down the driveway," Lathe stated into the line.

Sorbin growled under his breath. "Alexa was in a *BMW* in town with a couple of guys. Moving position to check." A couple of seconds later, Sorbin crouched next to Lathe. "Damn. I sure didn't expect a house call from her. Suggestions?"

Sorbin didn't expect to get an answer from anyone in the inner circle, so when none was forthcoming, he wasn't surprised.

"They're parking," Lathe warned.

Instead, Donny answered. "You and me head down there, Sorb. I'll play Jimmy's bodyguard, and he'll meet them as the head of the house. You're the butler and will offer refreshments."

"And if we can't trance them, I'll drug them," Sorbin murmured, liking the plan.

A low growl came through the line, but Sorbin couldn't tell who made it — Kinsey or Destrawn.

You better be fucking careful.

Sorbin smiled upon hearing Destrawn's voice in his mind. "Don't worry," Sorbin assured. "We got this. Besides, we wanted Alexa and Vynce alive. The rest are all expendable."

Sorbin had worked with Donny plenty of times. He knew they could pull it off.

"They're going to be just one of two distractions," Vicon warned. "You focus on what's going on in there. We'll take care of everything out here." His buddy's voice turned hard.

"No mercy."

As nice as it would be to be able to give the humans a second chance, Sorbin knew it just wasn't feasible. If they'd managed to catch one or two hunters alone, maybe. Unfortunately, with so many converging on them, Sorbin knew the best thing would be to take them all out, then create a false trail showing that the group had left the area and moved to a new one.

That's Lathe's area of expertise. He'll get it done.

"Four are getting out of the vehicle," Lathe informed. "One woman and three men."

"We're on it," Sorbin replied.

Then Sorbin sprinted to the door that led the stairs down from the roof. Donny met him there. As they rushed through the house in a blur of speed, they stripped their clothes. By the time they reached Sorbin's suite, they were both already to their underwear.

While Sorbin rushed to his closet, Donny grabbed his bags. In a flash, Sorbin was back in the front room, tying a tie and laying it under his suit coat. He watched Donny finish yanking his leather jacket on over his shoulder holster and sidearm.

"How come you didn't have that on upstairs?" Sorbin asked curiously as he led the way to Jimmy and Kinsey's suite.

Donny shrugged. "I wasn't supposed to be part of the action. What was the point?"

Sorbin knocked on Jimmy's door just as the doorbell rang. "You explain," he ordered, pointing at Donny, as the chieftain's mate opened the door and glanced between them.

"No need," Jimmy told them, tapping his ear. "I was listening."

Nodding, Sorbin streaked through the mansion to the front door, all the while praying one of the other mates hadn't been dumb enough to answer the door. To his relief, there was no one else in the hall. Sorbin took a second to straighten his hair and clothes, then walked sedately to the door.

Sorbin opened the door and glanced around the group. Adopting his best formal tones, he asked, "May I help you?"

Reginald's eyes narrowed. "Hey, I know you."

Well, shit. I hadn't thought of that.

"You're that fag from the deli," he continued belligerently. "What the fuck are you doing here?"

"I'm working," Sorbin replied calmly. Then he focused on the woman and the blond, buzzed-cut human, since he knew they were in charge. "May I help you?" Sorbin repeated.

Alexa snickered maliciously. "Well, well. Not only do we get to clear out the demons and their ilk, we get to kick out a fag, too." Her brown eyes narrowed with a malicious gleam. "I'm here to see your master, fag. Take me to him."

Sorbin arched one brow. "Do you have an appointment?"

"We don't need a fucking appointment," Vynce claimed, pulling a gun from beneath his jacket and pointing it at him. "Now, take me to your boss."

Lifting his hands in a placating manner, Sorbin used his foot to push the door wider. Then he turned and started down the hallway. "Master Aldemen will be in the sunroom at this time of day," he said by way of explanation as he showed them through the house. "This way."

When Sorbin walked into the room, he spotted Jimmy reclining on a lounger. He had a book in one hand and a drink in the other. The young human looked up and smiled at him.

"Hey, Sorbin," Jimmy greeted. "Who was at the door?"

As if that was a queue, Sorbin turned and grabbed Reginald's arm. He hauled him close, using the man's sideways momentum to turn him. In seconds, Sorbin used the human as a shield.

That didn't stop Vynce from pointing his gun at him and firing.

No honor amongst hunters.

Reginald screamed in pain and fear as Vynce continued to shoot him, as if hoping one of his bullets would fully pierce Reginald and hit Sorbin.

While Vynce was focused on Sorbin, Donny raked his claws through the third man's throat. Blood spurted, spraying streaks of red across the wall and everyone's clothes. Perhaps the hot liquid hitting him drew Vynce's attention, for he spun. Before he could begin shooting again, Donny grabbed the man's arm and squeezed, breaking the bones and forcing the hunter to drop his weapon.

"Stop now, or Aldemen gets a bullet in the head," Alexa ordered.

In an instant, Sorbin was on Alexa. He didn't show her mercy just because she was a woman. Grabbing her wrist, he forced it toward the ceiling. At the same time, he scraped his claws across her belly. Sorbin knew they wanted to capture her alive, so he didn't cut deep. Instead, it was just enough to cause her to scream, drop the gun, and crunch over on herself.

"You're demons. You're not supposed to be here," she whispered, glancing between him and Donny in horror. "How can you be here?"

Scoffing, Sorbin opened his mouth to give her a scathing response . . . but any sound was drowned out by the sound of roars. He shoved the injured woman toward Donny, who caught her easily, since Reginald had passed out, probably from pain. Then Sorbin braced.

A second later, Kinsey and Destrawn barreled into the room, both in their true forms, causing Alexa to faint.

Geez, these hunters are pussies.

Before Sorbin could greet Destrawn, he was hauled into his gargoyle's arms. "You're hurt!" his lover cried. "Where are you hurt?"

Sorbin realized how his soiled suit could look and quickly assured, "It's not my blood. I'm totally fine." As he spoke, he stroked over Destrawn's shoulders, hoping to soothe his protective beloved.

"I need to check," Destrawn declared, and Sorbin suddenly found himself swung up into his gargoyle's arms and being carried from the room.

Donny laughed from behind him, calling, "Don't worry. We'll take care of everything. Go have fun getting sexed-up!" More cackling laughter sounded down the hall after him as Donny yelled, "See you this evening for the party if you can walk straight!"

Even knowing it would be forever before he lived this down, Sorbin couldn't say he minded. After all, he was indeed about to be sexed-up, and he was going to enjoy every last minute of it.

Sorbin would always welcome his overprotective gargoyle's attentions . . . forever until the end of time.

YOU MAY ALSO ENJOY THE FOLLOWING FROM EXTASY BOOKS INC:

Interrogation Techniques
Charlie Richards

Excerpt

"You're coming, Del, and that's the end of it!"

Enforcer Delanrue Drudeson turned his head just enough to arch his left eyebrow as he pinned a side-eyed look on his youngest brother—Dakota.

"Seven," his brother continued. "And if you want that shit microbrew stuff you like, you can bring it your own damn self."

Delanrue—Del to his brothers and only his brothers—growled softly under his breath. It wasn't because he didn't want to go to his youngest brother's Christmas party. Actually, Del did.

Instead, Delanrue fought against curling his lip because he spotted Glade Kanston strutting down the corridor toward him. He found the other Shifter Council enforcer to be a piece of entitled, self-absorbed shit. Del had hoped he would be implicated in working with one of the rogue ex-councilmen, just so he could arrest him and never have to deal with him again.

Too bad that hadn't happened.

Glade was not only straight as an arrow with a stick up his ass, that stick meant he wasn't going to break any shifter laws, either.

Guess that's a good thing.

"I mean it," Dakota pressed, clearly misunderstanding his vocalization. He waved his finger under Del's nose while adding, "If you're not there by seven, I'll send —"

"I'll be there," Del stated in a low gruff voice. "Stop your bitchin'."

Del couldn't care less who Dakota thought he could send to get him to comply. If he didn't want to go somewhere, he wouldn't. The only time he did something he would rather not to was when he was ordered by the Shifter Council.

Seeing as Del loved his job as an enforcer and interrogator for the Shifter Council, that didn't happen too often.

"Good," Dakota replied, sounding smug. Then he must have spotted who actually held Del's attention, for he muttered, "Oh."

Del grunted, but left it at that, since by then, Glade had drawn close enough to be within earshot. Trying to avoid true interaction, he met the lion shifter's gaze and dipped his chin in the barest of nods. Then Del focused his attention down the hall past the man.

From the corner of his eye, Del saw that Dakota did much the same thing. Then his brother returned to their conversation, and Del knew it was a ploy to keep Glade from attempting to engage them. Especially since Del knew Dakota was already aware that he knew the information.

"Dane said he might be bringing a date," Dakota told him, a chuckle in his tone. "If he can convince the lady to join him, that is." With an open laugh, his brother added, "Guess our brother is having trouble convincing her that he's sincere."

"Probably because he's not," Del replied absently. Shaking his head, he thought about their middle brother's desire to date a human woman named Linda. "She's not his mate. I don't see why Dane is bothering. He can never reveal what we are to her, and he'll have to dump her eventually anyway."

Del had never understood why a shifter would date someone who was not only not a paranormal, but not their fated mate. There was no future there. Besides, even if they did decide to date a paranormal, Fate could place their mate in their path at any second.

Even though Del had warned his brothers of that very thing on many occasions, both of them had been in and out of many relationships over the nearly two centuries they'd lived. Del would sit back and watch, and when their liaison inevitably fell apart, he'd helped his brothers mend their hearts.

"Dane is dating some poor hapless woman?" Glade smirked, stopping to stand in their path. He even crossed his arms over his chest as if that would make him some immovable object. "I bet he hasn't even let the lady know he's a dick licker. Maybe I should swing by tonight and let her know."

Del twisted his lips into a scowl as he glared at Glade. "Watch your mouth, Enforcer Glade," he ordered. As the council's lead interrogator, in the intricate hierarchy within those working for the Shifter Council, Del's position topped the lion shifter. "Or someone on the council may hear about your slurs."

Glade tipped his chin up and attempted to look down his nose at Del and his brother. "I'm sure I wouldn't have anything to worry about. I work under Councilman Peregrine, after all," he stated, referring to an elk shifter who disagreed with homosexual matings. "He knows the true value of loyalty."

Councilman Georgio Peregrine's views had nearly caused him to lose his position, since he'd been backing other councilmen who were committing crimes against shifter-kind. When those crimes had come to light, the councilman had turned against them. That hadn't changed what he thought about gay matings, however. It just meant he was more subtle about where and when he voiced those views.

Evidently, he shares them with Glade.

Del knew better than to engage a bigot. Besides, he had places to be. He was in the middle of interrogating the last half dozen shifters who'd been captured when they'd taken down the now-deceased rogue ex-councilman Krakow.

Good riddance.

Taking a step to the left and forward, Del began rounding the idiot standing in the middle of the hall. He noticed Dakota doing the same to his right. He peered beyond the man, turning his thoughts to the upcoming interrogation he needed to do.

That morning, Del had picked the brains of two bear shifters and one tiger shifter. Then he'd stopped to have lunch with Dakota. His afternoon would consist of the last three men they'd found.

Finally, the dungeons would be empty . . . of those people anyway.

Del knew a few shifters had been brought in for other crimes, but they hadn't been a priority. The council wanted all the information they could on Krakow's contacts, so they'd focused on his associates. Unfortunately, the wolf shifter hadn't shared too much about his organization with his minions—probably because he thought they were beneath him.

I bet Pedro knows something, though.

Pedro Kenbrook had been Krakow's accountant for over a hundred years. He'd created false accounting information to hide his activities—payment for the sale of shifters as well as the money Krakow had paid to the mercenaries who captured them. Their cyber team had also uncovered files on the serums that the military was concocting by experimenting on shifters, although the formulas were incomplete.

Can't wait to make that guy crack.

They'd purposefully made Pedro wait until the end, allowing him to watch cell-mates disappear from around him.

"Hey, don't you walk away from me," Glade snapped, grabbing Del's upper arm. "I'm not done talking to you."

Del barely resisted rolling his eyes. With his thoughts on his duties, he'd nearly forgotten Glade was there. Pausing, he pinned the moronic lion with a cold gaze. "Not wise to put your hands on me," he stated, cutting a quick glance at where Glade had the audacity to touch him without permission.

Glade scoffed, although a hint of uncertainty crossed his features, but only for a second.

No sense of self-preservation.

"Like I said," Glade claimed. "You can't do anything to me. I'm Peregrine's favorite."

Del was damn tempted to sock the other shifter anyway. He couldn't give a shit that Glade thought he was untouchable. Seeing Dakota move to stand next to him and taking in his brother's angry expression, he knew the other male was way out-classed.

We'd wipe the floor with him.

That was exactly why Del resisted.

About the Author

Charlie started writing fantasy when she was eight, and after stumbling onto her first erotic romance at age nineteen, she realized her true calling. She now focuses on writing gay erotic romance, normally of the paranormal variety, with heroes of all kinds. With the help and support of her husband, Charlie finally fulfilled one of her life-long goals . . . move to acreage with her horses. You can often find her curled up with her laptop and a cup of tea or glass of wine, creating her next adventure. Charlie enjoys exploring the mountains of her new Oregon home on horseback, 4-wheeler, or motorcycle.

She can be reached at ch.richards2010@yahoo.com

Or visit her at www.charlie-richards.com